WINGS
OF
RED

WINGS OF RED

A Novel

JAMES W. JENNINGS

SOFT SKULL ✦ NEW YORK

Wings of Red

Copyright © 2023 by James W. Jennings

First Soft Skull edition: 2023

Library of Congress Cataloging-in-Publication Data
Names: Jennings, James W., author.
Title: Wings of red : a novel / James W. Jennings.
Description: First Soft Skull edition. | New York : Soft Skull, 2023.
Identifiers: LCCN 2023019127 | ISBN 9781593767099 (trade paperback) |
    ISBN 9781593767105 (ebook)
Subjects: LCGFT: Novels.
Classification: LCC PS3610.E55785 W56 2023 | DDC 813/.6—dc23/
    eng/20230502
LC record available at https://lccn.loc.gov/2023019127

Cover design by www.houseofthought.io
Cover photograph of buildings at dusk © Jason Koxvold / Millennium Images, UK
Book design by Laura Berry

Published by Soft Skull Press
New York, NY
www.softskull.com

Printed in the United States of America

10 9 8 7 6 5 4 3 2 1

To inspiration and patience

Whenever you take make sure to give back.

—BEAR PAW

CONTENTS

HOME

SCHOOL

HOME

1 / FORTUNE

My name's June. I'm a New City substitute teacher when they need me. What else is there? My lease is up tomorrow and quietly I still owe October rent. My two roommates, my godbrother, and I are shooting dice in the dining room. What else? Winter's approaching. It's almost bubble-jacket-and-long-johns season. The idea of roaming New City homeless is not something I'm looking forward to. I pick up the dice and roll. A win would be nice.

Cast of characters so far is my godbrother, Hollywood; the "blood brothers," Big and Blue; and me, June Papers, gambling off an upturned dining room table that's never seen a meal. What else? I'm about to see how much sacrifice I'll commit to to keep these dreams afloat. What else? First things first, I need spending money for food and transportation, and for that I need some love on the dice. I watch them spin and put a lowkey prayer up for the win. The landlord gave me all of September to try to find a way to pay what I owe in back rent. I tried my best. New City is ruthless. The ten-dollar bill under Hollywood's lilac loafer's my last. It's a $120 jackpot or nothing. Oh, lilac is like if purple and off-white had a baby. Two dice bound from the tabletop, colliding with the third.

Heeeell no. Hollywood flicks his toothpick. I realize that, to my younger readers, gambling for food and transportation is degenerate activity. I don't condone it. These are what we call extenuating circumstances. I know most of you've yet to pay a bill let alone rent and life is a race to grow older or a struggle for individuality, both ridiculous. I want you to know what I mean. Being wrong is inevitable. You'll be wrong a lot. What I'm asking you to do is make sure you give yourself the chance to see the thing through before you judge yourself permanently. Far too many people harm themselves because they don't have the time or space to see clearly. Perspective.

In my room there's a Malm bed, a big black desk, four white boxes of manila folders, and various notebooks I can't take with me. Sit on bed and trash a kaleidoscope of works that at some point seemed sacred. See what I mean? Perspective. I'm an artist. I'm a creative. I try to be honest with myself. Honestly, I feel like you need to be able to pay bills with a trade or, at the very least, get elevated by the people before you can claim it so for honesty's sake I'm a substitute teacher. Carry bedroom trash out front with the rest of our soaked belongings and watch a litter of street kittens wrestling in the vacant lot.

Yo! Big steps outside with a miracle in his eyes. *Uncle Grant said he buying one of your paintings.* I ask which one and try not to faint. Big sits on the top step and says he doesn't know but Uncle Grant's stopping by in the morning. I cover the trash bin, and Blue steps out with us. We watch the early night action from the stoop. Too soon to bank on the miracle at present, I entertain the possibility and carry on business as usual. If it's a larger painting, we can definitely afford to stay. Everything working out for that to happen is a long shot.

Sell him on a big joint. Blue. *Maybe we can keep the lease.*

The bigger the better. Big is cautiously optimistic.

But then there's next month, I reason. Murkt Street is our third New City apartment together, and as is often the case, the city takes far more than she gives. *We'll see.* The boys and I head back inside and argue Blackness, authenticity, and gentrification while finishing off some of Mom Dukes's homemade potato salad.

Last supper. Blue seems content.

Hope not. Big shrugs.

Lord knows I don't know. Thinking got me into this mess in the first place. A master's in fine arts. I've lost my sense of things. Say a prayer Uncle Grant buys a big painting and get a surprising surge of confidence. Walk to my bedroom for one last glorious nap.

Yeeer! Hollywood yells as he bursts through the front door. I rise to an orchestra of footsteps. *We got company,* he says. People often confuse Big and Blue because they're both tall and husky with on-and-off beards. And they're brothers. I've never heard anyone confuse Hollywood for anyone other than Hollywood. In classic form he choreographs a last magical night at 1497 Murkt Street.

Where do I know you from? I ask a bartender type whose head is buried in our fridge.

"Where's your food?" is a better question. She slides the empty bowl that held the potato salad. There's a black heart tattoo behind her ear.

We're moving out, I say. I don't know her name, but I recognize her. We're FaceCrook friends. After everyone's gone I scrape a couple years' worth of waxy gunk from the roof of the microwave.

It's therapeutic, 4:52 a.m., and keeps the mind afloat. I've moved enough to know not to grow too attached to any one place, but I feel sad about this one. I'm going to miss Murkt Street. I'm going to miss skateboarding around the house. I'm going to miss lying on the floor. Whoever laid the parquet in the front hammering nails top and bottom rotating and repeating eight planks per square was a genius. There are some water-damage warps and she gives here and there, but she will certainly be missed. I scrub the inside of the microwave one last time and have a bright idea. Run to the living room, grab my smaller paintings, and hide them behind our upturned dining room table. Hopefully that forces Uncle Grant to buy a big one. Lie down finally and stare at the white ceiling.

Uncle Grant never shows. Something about work. We finish packing and cleaning, and move on. The sun does what suns do. The boys rent a truck and store the beds, one I just traded to Blue, in a small storage unit a few blocks away. I have $120 in cash, a messenger bag, and a smartphone in my pocket. I have an idea of the life I'm supposed to live and the blankest of canvases ahead. Heart heavy and in my feelings a bit, we luck up on an art show our buddy Marty's putting on.

2 / DANGER

THERE'S RED VELVET CAKE, CHAMPAGNE, AND A DJ with good music. Doesn't feel much like a ledge at all. After the music stops and the cake's gone, the boys and I part ways. Figuring I might as well get a jump on surviving New City homeless, I leave first and avoid an otherwise long and sad goodbye. Fate and the weather align perfectly. The winds're ferocious. There's no storms worse than the ones you bring upon yourself. New City is no shelter. I stand under scaffolding and talk to a stranger because it's a bit less windy and lonely. Stranger leaves and I pretend I have some place to go too. Hang a right onto Broadway. Place my bag atop cast-iron steps and rest. Life is like this as well, I'm learning. Winds pick up speed and I carry on. Strange momentum takes me right back around to the gallery, but it's now closed. Lights out and locked up. Party done. Nobody but me.

I walk the block again to kill some time I assume. I sit on new cast-iron steps. Pick my bag up and return to gallery. In my heart there's a mix of rage and self-pity. In my head there's an odd game of thinking and trying not to think as I lap the strange block again. What appears to be a pile of dirty clothes morphs into a scribe nestling into darkness and leaves in the gallery step-down. *Snooze you lose.* Scribe sneezes into his sleeve. *Gotta keep it moving, kid.* I circle the block again wondering if God is talking to me through a stranger.

Maybe I should take a left, I say to myself as I watch buddy curl up into a cozy little ball. Reality hits me like the A train. My first real thought since leaving the party and it's crystal clear. I realize watching this sad drama play out that I half hoped to sleep where the scribe was now resting. *My goodness.* I take a left.

Carry on across the Broadway gusts and venture finally into the unknowable. Once my muse, my lover, my home, and my dream, New City's now my mysteriously unyielding mentor. What else is there? I keep walking. Luck up on a twenty-four-hour café for coffee and respite, find a seat by the window, take out my notebook, and make my offering.

I decide to journal daily now so that at the very least I'll be able to see whether my issue is as simple as me. As for the fiction this is it. Doesn't really matter what you call it once you live it. Against all good advice, my life and my literature are inseparable. I may be ashamed of my current predicament and embarrassed by the truth, but I'm 100 percent me, no matter what industry calls it. After a word or two it's all fiction anyway. At least fiction is honest about that. All that really lasts is the living and whether you opened yourself up to the heartfelt possibility of your unique experience.

That's my half-a-million-dollar education in fifty words or less that nobody asked for. Take care of yourself, don't spend too much time talking about other people, and live your own life, not someone else's. Teach yourself how to persevere, and pick up the rest on the way. So says the guy with no real next move except walking and wishing.

Finish café, pack up, and walk north with the strongest winds. I don't hear or see any news of hurricanes. What else? The writer voice in my head comes outside to play. Normally, I'd have to sit down and find a comfortable space to write, but floating as I am now, I hear sentences come forth and link up into paragraphs every few blocks. I can see them illuminated like sky-blue neons in front of me. Find another café and get the sentiments down to the best of my God-given ability. Ever since I was seven, my life goal has been to buy Nana and Ma a house. Two houses. I don't think this is unique to my situation, but it is true. As I pass New City night lights and the millions sleeping here and there, I wonder how it is I'm not a millionaire yet. Me being homeless is merely comedy until it dawns on me, listening to my own footsteps, that I've fallen for the pretty girl who can have whoever she wants. It's a strange thing not to realize until now. Drink another coffee. Out in the wind is just another cost of living, it seems, when you decide to do it your way and see the thing through. Whatever truths I can land and whatever fears I haven't faced under the late night of New City's twenty-four-hour cycle get the treatment. A couple hours with a composite journal plus nowhere else to go equals a lot of words. Jittery from the caffeine and a little paranoid, I pack my things again and head underground.

Express bulls into the station, displacing enough stale air for one to call it refreshing. It is not. Tall youth with white hair jogs off train and lobs a pink handball to the subway ceiling. It touches top and grosses her friend out. Pretty late for young ladies to be drifting. Germ ball bounces my way, and I kick it back. Blondie fields it and thanks me. Her eyes are dry-eraser green. A pair of rats race down into the tracks after train, and the girls squeal. The cheese the rats seemed to be fighting over is abandoned now on the platform. Rather than cheese, it turns out to be a frosted donut with holiday sprinkles. Every year five million children under the age of five die from malnutrition and starvation worldwide. In New City rats eat donuts. Blondie fans herself and faints into her friend's arms. I figure it's the rats until she wakes up. No one comes to like that. *Nothing like a true friend,* she says. It's a routine I gather. One friend runs, plants, and backflips out of another's lap. Great height. Between the eyes, the athleticism, and the choreography, they must earn. I don't give them anything because funds are low and I'm nobody's intended audience, but I'm sure they make bank. Local train slows to a stop and I hop on. A lone nut removes a block of literature from his backpack and rolls it around in front of his closed eyes as if reading by osmosis in a trance. I do my best not to stare as he keeps the literary block afloat with volleys of illuminating expressions imploding behind his elephant-print eyelids. Take out my notebook and mind my business. It's all so poetic.

3 / VISION

NEXT STATION ANOTHER SCRIBE WE'LL CALL JOE boards and sits between buddy and me. *Come on, man.* I stand up. The rest of the car's empty. Buddy doesn't seem to mind, but Joe's so worked over you can't tell a boot from an ankle. He smells like goat cheese.

For forty minutes I try to remember anyone who might owe a decent favor/family to beg. Though she's beautiful as ever, I'm not exactly in love with New City and the way she's been treating me lately. Aboveground in the Bronx, concluding this could be worse, I scroll though my contacts one last time. *Man up,* I say. Train back through Bronx I see I might need to lean more toward recklessness to follow through here. Pride in my manhood isn't nearly enough fuel for the night. What does that even mean at this point? Each stop has its own war to wage, and New City public transportation has no shortage of war-ready weirdos. I think I'm dreaming, but I'm not when I wake up in the car with my freshman-year roommate from undergrad. Can't recall his name, but I know it's him, so I take out my phone, stare into space, and rub my beard as if I'm doing something important. *It helps to remember,* I type.

Living is quite the adventure, the moon's whipping around us, we're ripping around the sun, and we hardly feel a thing. Roomie steps off at next stop, and I notice it's not even him. Frontin' for no reason.

Jump off the train before the airport for fresh air and a reset. No twenty-four-hour cafés, 3:47 a.m., I walk around. Halfway feel. Sounds like someone's following me. I stop to listen, but it's my own footsteps and a few distant cackles. Way more tired than afraid now. Walk in the middle of the street. The curb's high and there's no one out here but me. Stop in a bodega and buy a hot tea.

Tank you. Clerk hands over two quarters and picks up with his coworker.

You got a dollar or fifty cents I can bum? a raspy scribe asks.

I should be asking you.

Head back for the train. A woman enters the car through the emergency doors and settles past the cops and me. She smells wonderfully inebriated. I close my eyes and enjoy.

Wake up and train's at a standstill. Last stop, 6:58 a.m. I gather myself, shoulder my messenger bag, and walk out into a bright morning sun. It's not necessarily freezing, but it's definitely November 1. You can see the bull's breath out your nostrils. I trek Flatbush to the library and swipe my alumni card. Not sure I've ever been this type of tired before. Zombie-walk to the computers to check email and it feels like a dream. See a sale for $89 flights to Saint Timothy and remember summer there. Everything was so fresh and forgiving. Millions of free mangoes. I click through for fun and end up investing in a one-way. Nostalgia will buy you a ticket to recklessness. *Well,* I say to myself. Excited and exhausted, I drift to the second floor, find a good desk with outlets, and charge my cells.

4 / ODDS

AN INFAMOUS KICKBALL BOUNDS HIGH OVER A TALL park fence. Where the wobbly red orb will land is both impossible to know and half the fun of kicking it. The girls leak out, wrestling for choice real estate. For every excited smile there's an intense desire for this odd red ball to survive. Someone has to catch it. This much they know. One or two bounces and it is Third Avenue who decides whether the game shall go on. Third Avenue is neither kind nor playful. The girls brace themselves. Our wobbly old ball's been booted so many times she appears to be birthing another. As for flight and trajectory, it's a crapshoot.

Maybe deep down most Third Avenue males are good guys and if you were in a burning building they'd save you, but at street level from an educator's perspective, they're mostly vultures waiting for temptation to turn into opportunity. Peanut vendor wheels his cart closer. Maybe it's just the lure of the forbidden. Either way, construction workers, cops, and suits all seem to enjoy the allure of our wobbly red ball.

Gravity wins out, the girls brace with micro-adjustments, and the kickball plummets. Dancer girl whose name I forget makes the catch. Peanut vendor claps twice. Mid-celebration a boy in suede boat shoes steals the kickball, and a chase ensues.

Stay inside! I yell. Students take their time walking back through the gate. To the untrained eye it's just teenagers playing kickball. Fun and joy. To a homeless substitute teacher it's like watching another willfully blind bubble readying to burst. The alpha girls are stuck on saving the ball; Third Avenue chesters are all stuck on the girls for various repressed fantasies; the alpha boys are all predictably confrontational faux protectors and stuck on the girls. The other girls and boys are stuck on being like the alpha girls and boys and we day workers are stuck fully conscious in a strange game for chump change. My true job out here is to keep the chesters at bay and make sure no one gets hurt. Crowd control and chester protection. That's it. There is no teaching going on. I watch professionals walk by and allow themselves to get stuck wishing they had a chance to be teenagers all over again. Everyone does it. Everyone wants what someone else has until they have it. Then they want what someone else has. People take little stock concerning their own blessings. When there are teachable moments I'm all in, but they're few and far between. I mostly try to get the students to appreciate being alive and healthy with dreams. That's it. Twenty years from now I don't want them sitting here watching the same old tragedy play out again as if they've never seen it before or weren't at least warned. When I can close my eyes I make sure to enjoy the warmth of the sun.

I take attendance, pack up, and walk class back uptown to school. Today's easy money. I have to wait two weeks to get to it, and not much of it, but easy. Feeling free and strangely diligent, I walk downtown to the board of education to check the status of my full-time substitute license. Just as odd, I get an unexpected interview regarding my application. Touché, universe, touché. A nice and rather serious lady takes me to the back and goes through the motions. Clearly she has work to do. Reminds me of one of my aunts in South Carolina or Grandma Billings a bit. She pauses and squints at a notation on her screen, and I feel my worlds begin to swirl. I can feel it before she even says it.

I see you've had a previous conviction, she says.

I have. They told me that was expunged, though.

Board of education sees everything, she tells me.

I see.

She removes her reading glasses and asks what happened. I tell her the truth. She approves my application for final review. Bigger than the approval, though, is that when I was talking she was actually listening. It felt like some impromptu therapy in the last place you'd expect. What a nice lady.

Text Blue and meet him at a loft party on Dekalb. Lean against what I think is a wall and ends up being a sturdy little bookshelf. I'm that guy tonight. Felt like a wall. Collect the literature and get a slap to the back of the neck. Feels like a whale tail.

Sorry. She blinks too much. *I thought you were my friend James.* A few folks laugh as she pivots and walks off toward the kitchen. I pick the tough little bookshelf up. A couple paperbacks are stuck behind a record player I'm not reaching beyond. Already doing too much. Partygoers still looking, I find a way to care very little and gaze past them out the giant loft windows. I'm still shocked at how nice that lady was at the board of education. Maybe it was just that I needed to talk about what happened and she could tell or something. Either way, I'm feeling a great sense of gratitude and relief when I see the boys exit one of the room gatherings with coats in hand. I pick up and fall in line. Descend the tight flight of stairs and catch buddy we walked in with who wanted to buy a book hipster drunk at the bottom of the steps.

That's buddy from Public? A cheap restaurant bar downtown.

That's buddy we walked in with.

My goodness. He's splayed with his face to the ceiling like a starfish. *Did he even make it to the party?*

Who knows.

That's going to be a rough morning.

Hold that. Hollywood steps past.

"Hold that" means "sucks for you" or "better you than me." Same thing really.

I see a twenty-dollar bill peeking out his hoodie and trade him for a copy of *Strays. Strays,* or *United Strays of America,* is my first novel. I published it with what was supposed to be rent money a few years back. *Strays* is a cold press of my reckless sophomore year in college. I put my faith in it, fully convinced it would make me a millionaire. Feels like I've been behind on rent ever since. *Strays* has also morphed into much more than a novel. It's a business card. It's a living will and a conversation piece. I prop doors open with it. *Strays* travels with me. I sell copies whenever I can. Hollywood and Blue disapprove of my aggressive sales tactics. Row seems rather impressed. Step outside and hear a gunshot in the distance.

People are wilding, Row says.

Hollywood pats his pockets, concerned, and doubles back upstairs. I play numb and pretend the gunshots mean nothing too because I'm used to it, but I also know that it means a great deal that none of us have the words for yet. Hyper-present, no shower in two days, bullets flying, and I feel very alive. I get the sense that someone's watching us, but there's always someone watching you in the city.

We reach Blue's car and pile in. Something about four doors closing is soothing to me. Blue cues up some riding music and wheels out the park into a head-wrapped scribe who's now sprawled upon the windshield. Blue mashes the brakes, the scribe's front tooth pings off the windshield, and she tumbles onto the pavement.

5 / PING

WHAT THE— HOLLYWOOD SITS UP.

The scribe props herself up on an elbow and tugs at her front tooth.

Is this happening? Row chuckles involuntarily, if there is such a thing. Fight-or-flight mode fully engaged, I still have my hand on the door latch. Hollywood slaps his cell phone back together. Blue steps out into the drizzle and closes his door. We watch on as he and the woman exchange information and duck off into a bodega. *Pop!* Another mysterious gunshot. Someone having fun on a roof somewhere. Five long minutes later Blue hops in and adjusts his rearview. The indestructible scribe drifts back into the shadows of the park.

She's okay? Row asks. She's always had a genuine concern for people. Family full of doctors I think.

Good to go, Blue says.

I try to disguise my heart, but I'm still in fight-or-flight mode. I'm still waiting to see some lights roll so I can pop the door and run.

How much? Hollywood asks nonchalantly. Somehow he's been unaffected by all of this and is more concerned with his cell phone.

Blue steps out again, inspects the hood, and jumps back into the driver's seat. *I gave her an old metro card I already used twice and ten bucks.*

That's greeeease. Hollywood.

"Grease" = foul or opportunistic beyond the point of morality.

You lucky the glass ain't break. Hollywood smacks his phone like an old TV.

We drop Row off and head downtown. The accident shifts things. Whipping in and out of back blocks, Blue knows well I feel a lingering sense of numbness as I bob with traffic patterns. It's like I'm hardly here or powerless or merely an observer, and it's inexplicably empowering. Black-hole heavy. I'm at the mercy, life seems to say, of vehicles, people going places, and places driven by ideals. God knows what else. We pull up to the red light on Atlantic by Essence lounge and my immutable core takes control. My face, heart, and hands go airplane mode. I completely disassociate. It's a peace I can't recall feeling before. Feels like a fearless observation. I barely blink. It reminds me of the nothingness from which we came. Then it reminds me I've felt this nothingness before. I've felt it on my balcony overlooking a drop that would surely kill. I've felt it in college. I've felt it in adolescence. From nothing to a world of memories and expectations. A woman nearly killed me once. Did I already say that? I journaled about it not too long ago, but these last couple of days have been a blur. She and Ma were good friends when we lived in Meriden, and her boyfriend was a cop. We were over her place across the street, one thing led to another, and she pulled a pistol from her dresser drawer. She waved it over her head like a cowgirl and with a big smile put me in her sights. I was fourteen maybe and she didn't mean any harm I'm sure, but she was having fun with her finger on the trigger. I remember feeling the nothingness then. Later I heard she passed from breast cancer. A shame. I used to have a crush on her daughter. People can tell you all they want, but until you experience it and actually feel the shift to oblivion, the texture doesn't stick. Every time you could have died you kind of do. Youthful invincibility gives way to a cold logic and reason. You begin to understand probability and statistics. The light turns green and I drift off into Saint Timothy visions. I haven't told anyone, and I have no plan other than I'm going. For now it is good enough. I wanted to come up with Paris or someplace romantic, but all I could afford was a one-way ticket to Saint Timothy with a layover in Puerta Rica.

6 / WAKE

I HAVE A MASTER'S DEGREE IN FINE ARTS. I ALSO HAVE $100k in student loans and transgressions on my record that at times require explanation. As far as society's concerned, it's these two odd extremes that define me. There's no real context or content, but often these are the two notes that get bureaucratic gears to moving. There I am. June Papers. Twenty-eight years old. MFA with a felony. The classic young, Black, and gifted American misfit. It's too personal and whiny for the journal, so I ball an experimental page and shoot at the empty subway seats across from me.

I firmly believe that once you tolerate anything for a day or two, you can do it again and take from it what you will. I remind myself. I try to write into the future when all this in-between-leaseness will be a funny memory, but I sink instead into my present weariness like quicksand. I remember waking up two days ago and breaking the legs off my desk. I see the street cats playing king of the hill in the vacant lot next to our soaked belongings. I remember the girl with the heart tattoo in our fridge and the sound of the empty potato salad bowl.

At some point in my life the journey became the main character rather than the people or the bright ideas. More than the journey perhaps, it was my willingness to go. To dare. To create. To experience. Train life feels way more tolerable today. I see now why there are so many scribes on New City public transportation. Once you let the fear go or face it, the train's not bad. It's easy enough to find, there's usually a warm place to sit, you don't have to buy a coffee, and there's always entertainment. Scribes know a thing or two, man. Only problem for me is I can't bring myself to rest properly. There are too many stimulants, and I can't not pay attention, which makes me even more tired. Often you need art to take you places and inspire you. Other times, such as today, you need art to keep awake. I try to write it out. I've sat through enough workshops to know none of it's worthy of revisions. It keeps me awake. That's it. Maybe at some point these words will become literature, but right now it's smelling salt. Surf to the last stop, step off, and walk to the library. I hit the second-floor study desks and lay my head. Sleep here and there.

Rise out of hunger, count my monies, and train it back to good old Murkt Street for a hero. A "hero," for folks outside of New City, is a beautiful sandwich. Walking up to Maffia's bodega with hunger is like entering the warmth of the sun.

I no see you. Maffia slices the honey turkey from behind her fake glass fortress. Maffia's the Mother Teresa of heroes.

I level with her. *I been broke.*

She writes *$3.00* on the wax paper and nests it in a paper towel.

Okay. Tank you, she says. *I see you later?*

Yes, ma'am, I say. *Thank you.*

She smiles. One of my favorite paintings in the old apartment was a small portrait of Maffia. Take my hero up front, and Maffia's son rings me up from behind his fort of candy, cigarettes, and scratch tickets.

Three dollar.

Hand over my last twenty-dollar bill. The Jankees are playing on his small black-and-white television. Gives me time to pick up two small bags of chips. That's a business strategy somewhere. Probably the airport. Give people more time to wait, and they'll keep spending. I'm now down another fifty cents. For no good reason I imagine a single mother with three kids and get tempted to pocket some candy off principle. I don't, thankfully, but it segues into another bright idea of cashing the money order I set aside for Nana. Batter walks and Papi opens the register. *Fiiiive.* He lays down a five-dollar bill, thumbs through eleven singles, recounts, taps the stack, and plucks two quarters from the register.

You don't have nothing better than this?

He shrugs no. *Bess I can do, Papa.*

We have a brief stare-off, and I buy five Lucky Seven scratch tickets. Emotions are funny. I walk and scratch and win nothing as I pass an old neighbor smoking on her stoop. A bus turns down Murkt Street. A dog runs up and down neighbors' steps. See a little girl teasing dog as I toss the unlucky tickets in trash bin. Dog darts for the street as bus is barreling. Little girl chases dog. Inches short of her young life, the little girl's sixth sense kicks in and she freezes solid. Bus driver's oblivious. Mom beats little girl and dog.

Hollywood materializes out of nowhere. *Yeer! Shorty almost caught the pancake,* he says.

Mom snatches her up the stairs.

7 / SHOWER

HYGIENE BECOMES AN ISSUE. THERE'S A LAYER OF FREE living that starts to build after three days on the lam that's undeniably wild horse-ish. I'm walking to the library and detour to the gymnasium. I show the security guard my alumni card and he's unaffected. *There has to be a shower in here,* tell myself, passing the new vending machines. I dip downstairs toward the locker rooms. After the office and long benches there's a white tile room full of showerheads. Turn a lever and water flows. *Thank you, God.* One shoe off immediately, I pray for warmth. Drop my bag, undress, and prepare for the whatever. Strong and warm water turns hot. I hop in and get to scrubbing. Nice-smelling soap in the dispensers. Say what you want about oppressive student loans and a master's in fine arts, this peppermint-aloe body wash is amazing. I dry off with my day-one T-shirt and feel like a new man.

Weekends prove easier to navigate than weekdays. I stay up writing in twenty-four-hour cafés mostly. I nap and nod off wherever it becomes inevitable. I write to stay alert. With so many friends in the city, it's easy to find a couch or a floor to crash on.

The more you're willing to party, the easier it is to find a place to land. No one cares who stays where on Saturday. Sleepovers are encouraged. The only real problem is, it's taxing and tiring. Cheap thrills get expensive quick, and being in someone else's home is like being in their car. You kind of have to go where they want to go too. A couch is a nice comfort, and partying almost guarantees one sort or the other, but you don't want to suddenly have to make plans for whatever reason in the streets of New City on a Saturday night with all the creepers crawling.

Y'all out? I ask Blue as I tag a new notebook.

Bout to be. He checks the cover. *You still rolling?*

Yessir. Fist pump. We step out into the brisk city night.

Hollywood got a ride or he rolling with us? Blue starts the ignition. Take out phone, text, and see a colorful flash in my peripheral. *There he go.* A pigeon picks at a spilled dollar slice and surveys his domain. Blue snaps a photo. Row steps out with Hollywood.

Ay, I told Row we'd drop her off if it's cool.

Of course. Blue unlocks the doors. *We meet again.*

Row and Hollywood jump in. *Hey! Hey!*

Watch what you say around these two, Hollywood warns Row. *I'm not saying who, but somebody up front is working with the feds. They'll serve you up.* It's a game we play where everyone except you is a fed or a rat.

Plot thickens. I implicate Blue.

Yeah, aight. He wheels us through another New City night to Row's brownstone.

Thanks for the ride. She smiles.

No problem, Blue says.

Watch out for them crackheads, Row warns us. *Oh!* She ducks back down. *Do you all like movies? I have a box full from my job that I'm trying to get rid of.*

What? Hollywood. *Who doesn't like movies?*

Blue snipes a park, parallels, and we follow Row upstairs.

Welcome. She keys her door.

Hollywood shivers with joy upon entering. *It smells heavenly in here.*

My first thoughts are fresh linens and cardamom.

Row laughs. *I think it's the candles.*

She tidies up as we play the couch.

I wonder where she work at?

She's a producer she said. I'm proud of her coffee table literature.

Hollywood handles a big moving box. *We might as well take the whole thing,* he re-grips. *You work at Blockduster?*

She laughs. *I'm a producer. People send us stuff all the time.* She rearranges magazines I've disheveled. *Do you all want something to drink?*

I'm cool.

No thanks.

I'll take a water, Blue says.

We end up watching the first half of a romantic comedy, feet up on the coffee table with blankies and buttered popcorn.

This is not how I imagined the night would end. Blue laughs, somewhat confused. *What just happened?*

Hollywood points an argyle toe at the heroine. *She wants to commit, but she knows he's not ready.* Rubs his eye.

Are you crying?

Please. He laughs. *I'm trying to stay up.*

Must be the candles. I smile.

Blue has to make an uptown move, and Hollywood and I crash at Row's. Hollywood finagles the guest room, and within minutes it's just me sitting in the dark of the living room tired and excited to melt. I'll never underestimate or neglect comfort again. I'm drifting into a warm fantasyland, and my soul snatches me up out of it and forces me to write. The last thing I want to do is relive and transcribe what happened today, but I do. I finish with some cleverness about tomorrow being neither here nor guaranteed and forcing myself to write.

Wash my hands and give face and pits a decent scrub. Being lammy makes you think you're worse off than you are. I have a good face. I could smile more. At least twice a day I should work at being happy, I decide. I should shut the bully in his attic and at least twice a day I should let my inner five-year-old rock out till it's night night. Brush my teeth and head back to the living room.

First thing to pop up on this television is exactly what we're watching. Power on the remote, and electric-blue light paints the apartment. It's the guy with the brown beard who interviews all the actors.

At what age did you become homeless? he asks.

The studio audience is locked in.

I was seventeen when we moved from the city, actor replies. *Twenty when I stepped out for myself.*

I sit up and reach for my phone. I stop myself and relax.

"Homeless" is too strong a word. People get offended when you say it. Even though it's what you are. He works his craft. *Homeless? Noooo. Not you! They don't want to believe it. So I lied or talked around it.*

Interviewer rubs brown beard. *Until you become the highest-paid actor. Ever.*

Hands up touchdown. *Until then.*

The symmetry is almost lost on me I'm so relaxed and comfortable. My phone vibrates. Text request from the school secretary, Maggy, asking me to sub Monday. I thought I powered my phone off. Text back, *I'll be there.* Hollywood steps out the guest bedroom.

You still up? He opens the fridge and takes a carton of orange juice to the face. *What's the matter? You need a bedtime story?*

This dude made a hundred million dollars last year, I tell him.

Must be nice. Hollywood yawns. *Aight, bro.* He starts back. *Link me in the morning before you kick off.*

Bet.

I wish you could smell this apartment. I'm going to find a way to embed the pages with scent because it changes everything. On cue Row steps out.

You want one pillow or two? she asks.

One's fine. I thank her.

She disappears around the corner and returns with pillows and a blanket. *There's food in the fridge. Help yourself to all of it, please. Cups might be in the dishwasher.*

I got you. Thanks, Row.

Of course. Night night. She smiles and walks off.

I fold a pillow in half and lie out on the floor. The studio audience applauds. Actor shakes hands with brown-bearded interviewer. It's a small, subtle moment, but I appreciate it. It makes more sense now why I had to stay up.

8 / YOUTH

FIVE DAYS LATER, WALK UP TO THE SCHOOL, 6:37 A.M., and get a jump on life. Middle school today, so I have to prep a bit. I didn't even know New City had a middle school until a month in. I'm lying. I just wasn't paying attention. At first, I was only here two or three times a week helping Hollywood with basketball. One day the front elevator was down and we had to take the back with the middle schoolers. Once I started subbing consistently I realized how much of a difference a few years makes. Subbing high school is like filling in for a teacher. Subbing a middle school class is like filling in for a parent. Middle school substitute teachers should be paid time and a half if not double.

Exhibit A (for today): Two students fighting over a seat in the auditorium. Hundreds of seats in the auditorium, yet there's conflict over one. Must be a special seat. Looks normal. Any class in the auditorium is a recipe for lawlessness, but there are several hundred seats. Guilty smiles continue to butt-wrestle. I'm sure one is more wrong than the other, but that's not my concern. My job here is crowd control and public safety. You let one fight go, and you wind up with a riot. Usually it's the aggressor pointing the most condemning finger who's guilty. Luckily for me, the aggressor is also someone I can expect leadership from. Someone I can be disappointed in. He wants to play basketball.

I have to write a statement? baller asks.

Hey, man. It's an incident. I'm just following protocol.

He's hesitant at first, and then he pens the following gem:

> *Coach told us to find a seat and Cory was sitting in my seat. I told him to move and he gave me my backpack and tried to act like he didn't hear me. He said "what" mad times and I kept saying, "Get out my seat." Calmly. Coach got mad and asked us how many seats there were. He made us count all the seats in the auditorium and when our numbers didn't match he got all frustrated and told us to count again. We counted all the seats in the auditorium, which some could call corporate punishment but I'm not trying to rat (like some people). We were almost done counting and Coach got mad again because we were working together trying to solve the problem ourselves. Coach told us how many seats there were and asked why we fighting over one? I tried to tell him Cory stole my seat but Coach told us to write this instead. I was trying to tell him this isn't fair but he just went back to writing in his little notebook.*

The rest of the period is uneventful. Education at New City Public, which is set smack between midtown and downtown, is accompanied by the city's endless soundtrack. A lot of sirens and unnecessary yelling. I help break up a fake fight in hallway and begin to climb the stairs to get my screenplay critique from Priya, the eleventh-grade humanities teacher. Step out of the way of a pair of runners and continue my slow climb. Priya told me about a competition two weeks ago, and I missed the deadline, but luckily she agreed to read my screenplay.

The front elevator stops on 6, and I consider hopping in until an angry teacher stomps out.

I'm not going to say it again. His cheeks are flushed. *If you are NOT a teacher and you do NOT have an elevator pass, get OFF the elevator!*

Nobody moves. A few students look around for someone else to make a move.

I'll wait. Teacher holds the door. *I'm extremely patient.*

New City Public, like many New City public schools, is an overcrowded vertical building with a front elevator at its heart. The gym is on the tenth floor, the cafeteria is on the ninth, and the art room is on the first. Imagine having gym then art then lunch. The elevator is essential for all. Accordingly, there are strict rules as to who can use the elevator when, which change enough for me to avoid using the elevator as much as possible.

I'm getting off at the first floor, a young lady says. *'Cuz that's my stop.*

Do you have an elevator pass?

Are you my father?

Excuse me. He's looking at me. *Can you ask Mr. D. to call school safety, please?*

I pretend I never heard of a Mr. D. or school safety.

Misteeer, a jock pleads with the teacher. *I'm not saying a lot, but a little bit, you wildin'. I'mma be dumb late for no reason.*

"Dumb" means "very" or "extremely."

OD, another student adds.

You aaall should have thought about that before having a food fight on the elevator. Teacher looks to me again for some sign of life.

They threw a french fry. It is not that serious. Nobody had a food fight.

Now all of a sudden you know what I'm talking about. He crosses his arms. *Who threw it then? Who threw the fry?*

Crickets.

Sir. He's looking at me again. *Can you call for security, please?*

Sorry. I got caught up in the action.

I threw the fry. Okay? Jock says, obviously lying. *You caught me. Tell Mr. D., security, or whatever. Just let the doors go, please. We been on this elevator for like twenty minutes.*

Teacher looks at me one more time with a bit of disgust/disbelief, checks his watch, and lets the doors go. I carry on to Priya's classroom, knock, and walk in.

I just called for you, she says. *Ready?*

Ready. Never ready for workshop. Waiting to hear how many crimes I committed. How uncouth. How unrefined.

Good. Priya smiles kindly. *Let me finish this last essay.*

Take your time. I peruse her library.

How'd your day go today? she asks.

Sixth-grade drama class. They're always doing the most and none of it is clever enough to be funny, but everything's a joke.

Get some writing done?

Nod yes.

Priya opens her laptop and I sit next to her.

Okay. What I did was go through and make notes, which I'll send to you when we're done. I have a couple of big-picture questions that I want to ask you before we get started.

Make it more realistic/believable she says without saying. There were bright spots of course, but anyone can muster up bright spots with thousands of words.

Take the back stairs down to the second floor and walk in on the after-school folks getting audited by the board of education. Tension's a little high. I beeline for the supply room, which has become my unofficial bunker/locker.

Sorry. Walk by and close door behind me. *Let's see, let's see.*

Felicity walks in. *You can't be serious right now, June!*

What happened? I freeze up.

She mugs me in silence for a few seconds. *I'm just playing.* She breaks character. *I'm bored, yo. This lady's a stalker. Okay.* Felicity opens the door. *That's it.* Closes it behind her.

I lay my messenger bag down on the big black speaker and make two stacks of *Strays*. I quickly change into a fresh V-neck, undies, and socks, drop Nana's money order in a manila envelope so it doesn't get worked over, and make sure I'm decent to step out.

I wonder if anyone can tell I've been wearing the same 549 jeans for forever and realize it's not worth the time. Hollywood does a rat-looking-for-cheese face as I pass.

O.J., the school safety agent, smirks like I stink. *Where you sneaking off to?* She sees the manila envelope in hand, opens her top drawer, and hands me a letter. *Thanks. And Hollywood looking for you.*

I just seen him. They getting audited. I make a spilled-milk face. *Hold that.*

Right. Be right back.

I guess I should roll call the school crew. Those I know at least. You got O.J., the cutie who sat by the door, and Vio for school safety. In the main office you got Maggy, the school secretary, who does too much of everything; Clarissa on payroll; and Marie in attendance. In the after-school office you got Hollywood and Felicity from the Bronx. For teachers, there's Dexter the athletic director/gym teacher. Pope teaches history and heads the teachers' union. Priya, whom you met, speaks about seventeen languages. For math you got Trags, who can pie chart 99 percent of all rap lyrics. I think that's it. Oh, Anthony teaches a dope sociology class called Normal Is Weird with all types of tech integration. They might not realize it, but the students at New City Public get an impressive education for free. The middle school feeds well into the high school, so there's a wealth of peer-to-peer learning off the books, which is probably more valuable than all the curriculum combined. Thanks to Maggy, I've subbed all these classes. Upon exiting the building, I see Don, the high school director, and Lacey, the principal.

You out of here? Don asks.

Going to the post office. You need anything?

I'm okay. Thanks.

Lacey waves.

9 / NEXT

POST OFFICE IS AWFULLY QUIET FOR A THURSDAY. I hop on a short line. The two-story windows let in a ton of light, and the post office feels more like a cathedral than anything. It's possible it could have been one at some point. New City changes so much so fast. A worker shuts off his lane light and exits stage left.

The last employee standing dishes out change and a receipt. *Next!* he yells.

An older gentleman with liver spots removes his Vietnam vet cap and places a trophy on the counter. *I'd like to m-m-mail this to my grandson in Cincinnati, Ohio.* He stutters. *I have the address already memorized.*

Worker scans the people in line. *You have to get a box to mail it in.* He scratches his eyebrow. *You can try to wrap it for extra protection and get some packing peanuts, but you're going to want some kind of box first.* He points past the line. *Check the kiosk for what size.*

Oh. One second. Vet hurries over.

Lady on her phone is not happy. *You have got to be kidding me,* suit beats her to it. Postal worker gives us a blank look. Sympathy perhaps.

You pack it yourself, he says. *I can't help with that.*

Cell phone lady gets proactive. *You have to fold the box together yourself. He can't help you.*

Oh. One second. The vet makes a quick mess out of the situation. He's got the old-school hearing aids that look like a baby in the fetal position.

Short suit tries not to lose it. *Are we really serious right now? They need someone on the floor to help him, not the goddamn cashier.*

Resilient, the vet manages to get the box in shape finally and drops it back onto the counter.

Postal worker looks on in blank-stare amazement. *Sir,* he says calmly. *You need to tape it too.*

You don't have any tape back there? the vet asks.

We have tape for sale at the kiosk. It's four bucks with tax.

Oh, just give him some tape for Christ's sake.

No, the vet says proudly. *Ring me up for that.*

Postal worker scans the tape and the peanuts.

That'll be seven dollars and eighteen cents.

That's not bad for Ohio.

That's for peanuts and tape. The box is free, but you have to pack it and tape it before you pay for shipping.

Multiple death stares.

Cell phone lady squeezes the velvet rope like a stress ball. The suit has somehow managed to disassociate, and now I'm getting frustrated. My phone buzzes.

Hey, Nana. I'm sending the money order now. There's a . . . line at the post office. What's wrong?

Nana's crying and trying not to and arguing with Brook at the same time, so hard to tell what's what at first.

What's the matter, Nana? I ask as I step out of line.

Turns out the bank raised her monthly mortgage payment and she can't afford it.

Did you talk with the lady who helped with the refinance? I ask. A refinance is when you first negotiate terms for paying whatever you owe the bank on the property. *No? Call her back first.*

She tells me she been calling but hasn't heard anything and the bank is threatening to take the house.

No one's going to take the house, Nana. That's illegal. I pretend I know. *Call and then call me back.*

The vet's still taping his box at the counter.

Short suit reenters angry land. *This is in-sane. I'm on break.*

I step outside for some fresh air and the world rushes in. Lexington Avenue pigeons migrate overhead and it's both disgusting and beautiful. Hold my breath as they pass. A sports car growls down Twenty-Third.

My phone buzzes again. Joy, my sister.

What in the world? I answer, assuming she knows.

Oh Lord. She laughs. *What happened now?*

I tell her.

I can't, she says. *I gave them money last week and a few months ago. I don't know what's going on in that house, but I can't.*

Man. I try to figure the best way to move forward. Still pretty numb, I tell Joy I'll try to figure something out and call her back. Hang up and forget where I'm going and what I'm doing. A thousand suits swim past with a thousand more approaching. A jolly bunch mobs the hot dog vendor outside the methadone clinic.

I mean, listen, one suit says into his phone, *times are hard out here, my friend. I'm thinking about selling the condo in Miami.* Suit bumps me in passing and apologizes with a halfhearted wave. *Listen, bro.* He laughs. *I said I'm thinking about it.*

When I return the post office line's twice as long and the vet's peeling tape off his box.

It's for security reasons, Malkovich-looking postal worker says.

Security? The vet stands straight. *I served this country for thirty years! I can't mail a damn trophy for security reasons?*

Postal worker apologizes multiple times as the vet walks off, defeated.

Where's your tape? I ask.

Fuming still, he fishes it out the pocket of his bomber jacket.

I uncap a pen. *What's the address?* I write it as he tells me.

Thank you, young man. He smiles.

I smile back. *No problem. Now you'll know for next time.*

For reasons beyond me, the vet turns with his box and exits the post office. Maybe he was too embarrassed to continue here. Either way I get back on line. Moving like clockwork now. I place my padded envelopes on the counter half expecting vet to walk back in and try to cut me.

Feels like books here. You want to do media mail? clerk asks. *Should save you a few bucks.*

Yessir. I never heard of it, but it definitely saves me a few bucks. *Thanks.*

You're welcome. Next!

The sun is sharp and prickly on the walk back to New City Public. I see an 11/11 memorial ad lit up golden yellow, and a light goes off. My college buddy Hen and I sold flags on the first anniversary of 11/11 and made a few hundred bucks off it. As if I needed more clarity, I field Nana's call and get an exact number to aim for. The little billionaire in my brain takes over my legs, and we end up at a Party Arty store near Union Square.

I'm looking for American flags, I tell the cashier.

Aisle three, she says.

Hustle over as if someone's going to buy them before me and load cart.

Interested in a candy Rubrix Cube? Cashier pushes a promotion.

No thanks.

You're missing out. She rings up my flags. *That'll be sixty-four dollars and eighty-five cents. You want a box or a bag?*

Bag's cool.

By the time I get back to New City Public, O.J.'s gone, Vio's in her place, and janitors and after-school are running the building. Immigrant construction workers shuttle scaffolding planks onto the front elevator. I stash my flags in closet and stop by art room to use whiteboard to try to figure out the math. Eleven hundred over two weeks equals how much per day?

$$14 \sqrt{\$1,100} = 7$$

One tweeenty.

$$14 \sqrt{\$1,100} = 78$$

One tweeelve.

$$14 \sqrt{\$1,100} = 78.5$$

A worker jackhammers a floor above. *Let's say eighty.* Eighty bucks a day for two weeks. *I can do that.* I sit back and map it out. One foot in front of the other. As more immediate needs begin to circle down for a landing, I let myself loose to it all for a bit and find a dope piece of art in an animal book of an eagle, wings spread, with its talons in a rabbit. Take a flick with my phone and carry on into another New City night.

Wake up in a café to my phone vibrating. Look and see a flight check-in alert for JFK to STT. I'm still so dream/awake discombobulated and loopy that it doesn't feel quite like reality, so I pocket my phone and debate coffee or tea. Phone vibrates again and see it's Maggy.

Sub today? Four days actually?

Happy about the four days, I feel a lingering feeling, unpocket phone again, and see above Maggy's text this flight check-in alert for JFK–STT. Sounds insane, but I completely forgot. Suddenly faint, I stand and force myself to take deep breaths. I'm exhausted and my legs're rubber.

I've learned to follow my gut in big life moments, but my intuition seems to be taking a personal day today. I'm acclimated to the lifestyle and can walk for two hours if need be before a café break, but no amount of steps helps with the confusion. Even the city is no assistance. Rather than storefront fantasies and storied buildings, I see bright, unattainable trophies inscribed with a language I can't read. I may as well be exiled in a foreign country here. I imagine all the mangoes I can eat in Saint Timothy simply by walking up to this tree or that and plucking.

First light bleeds into the sky and I'm heading back to New

City Public texting Maggy when it hits me that I'm probably not going to Saint Timothy.

See Hollywood waiting at the doors for security. *Morning, bro,* he says.

It's bull's-breath cold again.

We throwing a loft party in SoHo Friday. Hollywood gets excited. *Should be a good time.*

That's a bet.

You not going. He laughs. *I can tell just how you said that.*

Cold, coffee-toting teachers walk up behind us, and O.J. opens New City Public for business. Hollywood and I elevator up to the gym.

Yo. I shoot a midrange. *If you had the opportunity to move to Saint Timothy today, would you?*

For what?

For what? It's eighty-eight degrees with mango trees.

I mean, I guess. He pulls a three.

That's a no.

Prolly not. I like the winter fashions, though.

Peanut sneaks in through the rear door and steals the rock from Hollywood. Peanut's one of our favorite middle school students.

How come every time I see you, you not in class? Hollywood asks.

It's morning advisory, Coach. Relax. Peanut shoots a three.

You subbing for us today? he asks me.

I am not. Thank Jesus.

Why you say that?

Middle schoolers don't listen. You have to say everything thirty times. High school is clockwork.

I can see that.

I bet you can. Go to advisory.

Let me get one last shot?

Only if it's midrange. I pass him the rock.

Peanut pump fakes, steps back, and shoots a three. Cash.

That's valid. Hollywood chases the ball down as Peanut exits victorious. *So you thinking about moving to Saint Timothy or that's a definite?*

Honestly, I bought a one-way with the bread I won off that dice game in the dining room and damn forgot about it. Until today, I confess.

I mean . . . Hollywood does some mental math and shoots a midrange jumper. *You doing a lot just to stay in the city right now, so I'm sure you'll be aight with whatever you decide. You just gotta decide. Rock, paper, scissors–type joint.*

Yeah. By lunch.

You got a half day? He gets jealous. *How you always get the half days?*

Hit the computer lab on a hunch and search Saint Timothy online newspapers for a housing or work-related miracle, happy my intuition has returned. No such luck. Sub first block of gym classes without major incident. For my free period I treat myself to dollar slices before the New City lunch rush and call airline to see about a refund. No dice, they say. Too late. Hit the after-school supply closet and thumb through my legal/important folder. Hollywood walks in laughing with half a peanut butter sandwich.

What you looking for? He turns on the light.

My passport.

You don't need a passport for Saint Timothy, do you?

I remember he's right but look it up to be sure.

So you going, huh? Hollywood asks.

I think so. I pack like a madman. *I was going to flip a coin, but I'm pretty sure I'm making the right decision. What you think?*

Follow your gut, my G.

We dap.

Hit me when you touch down.

Of course.

Time of the essence, I sneak out without saying too many goodbyes and train it to the airport. Watch a couple of nerds solve the same Rubrix Cube multiple times each. Breeze through security check-in and arrive at the departure gate as first-class passengers are boarding. Gives me plenty of time to buy some airport extortion snack and breathe the first breaths of relief in quite some time. Flight attendant announces my zone and I get giddy boarding the plane. Relieved, excited, and happy I decided, I chew on a red licorice straw in my window seat. There's an eerie quiet around me as if the universe is trying to say something I assume to be good until it hollows out into nothingness. I see people talking but hear only whispers. I feel outside myself as I remember Nana and the house. I can't leave.

10 / STAY

EXCUSE ME. I STAND, PASS MY ROW MATE, AND HEAD for the exit. *'Scuse me.* Run the aisle past first class and exit the plane. I run the breezeway and trigger all types of national security concerns I'm sure. Door still open luckily, I tell the stewardess what happened so as not to delay the flight. I would call the feeling gratitude for the sudden clarity as I watch planes coming and going, but I feel numb and tired honestly. Numb and tired.

Train back in New City and end up in the Fifties and Sixties by Center Park facing high-end shops and tourists, feeling sorry for myself as day turns to night. The candy-coated storefront charm returns a bit, but they still feel more like unattainable trophies in a language I can't read. By last light I feel better. New City nights energize. I wish I could've found an easier way to do it, but I'm glad I decided to stay. On cue a glittery storefront matrix lights up. Also on cue a vagrant removes his pants and urinates into a fast-food cup. Cop car pulls over and driver taps his partner, who's already shaking his head. *That's one collar we won't be making.*

Saw God in that sheepdog Sheila, vagrant howls to the stars. *I love yooou! Aw aw oooh!* He steps back into his pants. *I want my goddamn dog back, gotdamnit,* he says, slow-turning a dark corner past the bright matrix.

I shoulder my messenger bag and carry on. New City nights belong to the hidden desires. The creatures take over. I 5-train it uptown toward Westchester and the Bronx. Bag in lap, I cross my arms and lay head. Feel a kick on my leg.

Last stop, voice says.

I pan up the towering dark mass and see a slick-hair cop with an arm full of tattoos.

Last stop, he says again.

I see, I say.

He sizes me up and moves on through the car doors. Take my notebook out and write what I can remember from the past few hours. I watch through the window as he does the same routine with another scribe, who staggers off the train sans right shoe. Cop boots it off train onto the platform. Scribe's unaffected. Looks a lot like buddy who stepped out of his pants under the bulb matrix in Center Park.

Train doors close as an early-bird suit couple step on just in time. A fully charged Metro preacher enters at next stop, preaching a gospel of faith and pilgrimage. One perk of not going to Saint Timothy is I can somehow hear the white-sand beach waves in my head as if I'm actually there. It's as if I've learned to be two places at once. Imagination on steroids. I can feel the sun on my shin hairs. Taste the salt water on my lips.

11 / DUST

THE AFTER-SCHOOL'S SHOPPING CART IS SQUEAKY AND probably stolen. I push it across Twenty-Third toward the Madison Park suits all buzzing around and looking important. *I need a nice suit,* I say to myself. An electronic wheelchairer does about twenty past me, long blond hair near straight in the wind. *Slow down!* I yell, unfolding the white table. I dump the Party Arty flag bag and arrange the flags to sell. Too late to be nervous, I force myself to push forward.

Flags here! Getcha flags here! I yell as the suits carry on about their business. A New-City-T-shirt-wearing tourist walks up. Notice he has an Obama button on his vest.

How much? he asks.

Two dollars for the small ones. Three. I point to the medium. *And five. Free lit too.* I hand him a packet of artsy pictures and literature I put together for times like this.

Tourist seems genuinely intrigued by the work and buys two flags.

Thank you so much, I tell him. *Have a great day.*

God bless, he says.

As an artist you can spend so much time in a valley of disconnect that it can be a bit jarring and bizarre when you have a real human connection. I carry on with new spirits, but no one buys anything or even stops for over an hour. Business is funny like that.

What are you selling flags for? a voice asks.

Close my journal and get back to it. *The 11/11 memorial's tomorrow.*

Oh, that's right. He shows mixed emotions. *I'll take a few of those, thanks.*

Hand over mediums.

Suit kicks off and a Black cop approaches. *What type of freedoms we expressing here?* he asks.

Freedom of speech, of course. You can't sell goods on the street in New City without a permit unless they fall under freedom-of-speech works like art and literature.

I see, I see. You in college?

I am not. Hand him a free lit packet. There was a major turning point in the editing of *Strays* where I realized I had to get rid of most of the political ideas and social commentary. It killed the momentum of the story. Rather than trash it, I turned some into artsy essays and made a lit packet knowing it could help market *Strays*. *I have my master's in literature and fine art,* I tell him. *It's a terminal degree.*

He buys a small flag. *Smart,* he says. *Keep on, brother.*

Thanks. I will.

There's a slow burn of sales. Spotty. Nothing to get excited about but well worth the effort. As the sun begins to set I muse over the now infamous $400m question. What would you do with

$400m? How would you spend it and what would change? Come to the conclusion I'd get bored with spending after the first $100m. *What would you do then?* I ask myself. What would you do after you did all the things you always wanted to do? You can easily live off a portion of the interest. What charity would you donate to? What do you eat for breakfast the morning after you've had everything you've ever wanted to have for a month even?

I pack the rest of flags, break down table, load the squeaky cart, and head back to New City Public. It's a funny question because most people think no such breakfast will ever exist.

I'd have lobsters and shrimps and steaks and cupcakes, they say.

And then?

And then caviar and strawberry shortcake and all the food they can think of.

And then?

Most folks' desire is so strong that they can't see through to the inevitable. You will at some point, far sooner than you think, have everything you ever wanted—and you will be bored. Approaching New City Public, I conclude that I'll pretty much keep doing what I'm doing except I'll have more time to write and paint and be creative. I'll play a lot of ball, eat super healthy, and create a world-class artist studio/residency program to live and work out of. I'm visualizing it when O.J. steps out the door.

How'd we do? she asks.

Not bad. Sold about fifty flags.

That's great, bro. Congrats. I want my ten percent by Friday.

What are you still doing here? I ask.

They got a save-the-whales peace rally or something in the auditorium. Overtime, basically.

I understand. Carry on and stash up in the supply closet. Count the monies. *Two hundred and ninety-six?* Recount. Two hundred and ninety-eight. Even better. Stash, take out some petty cash, and log the progress.

$$\begin{array}{r} 1,100 \\ -238 \\ \hline 862 \end{array}$$

Walk to Burlinton Surplus, inspired to buy a white button-down and see Hollywood as I'm going to pay in the sneaker section. He's got one gold loafer on foot and a pair of purple runners in hand, summoning the footwear spirits it seems.

I creep up on him. *Give me all your discontinued sneakers.*

Ohoooo! I knew I seen a faux-hawk in aisle nine.

We laugh, dap, and hug.

What's good? I ask.

Chillin', bro. 'Bout to cop these joints and hit Public. What you doing? He inspects the dress shirt. *I thought you would be in Saint Timothy by now.*

I had to dead that. I forgot I have to get this money up for Nana real quick. I tell him about the flag selling and the malaise. *People not even patriotic anymore.*

Hollywood shrugs. *11/11 was like ten years ago.*

Damn. Time does fly after a while. We make our way to the cashiers and catch up. *Speaking of ten years ago, you know you still own me sixty bucks?*

You sure? I could have sworn I paid you that back.

I'm sure. I remember money.

I believe you. Matter of fact, I got you soon as I get my check.

As you buy loafers. I put him to task.

I mean, if you really need it now I can—

Nah. I need it by next week, though. Nana mortgage is through the roof.

I got you. So no Saint Timothy at all? Poo-poo face.

The Burlinton line is horrible, but we endure.

Now I need to raise like eight hundred dollars. Bug eyes. *Pretty much.*

Damn.

You said it.

A kid with a mohawk loses his balloon above the jewelry section. Line inches ahead. I buy my $26 button-down, Hollywood cops his loafers, and we head toward Astro Place. Phone vibrates, Maggy asking me to sub another half day. Lucky me.

How's the writing coming along? Hollywood asks.

It's tough out in the wind. All I do is journal pretty much, but more words than ever.

You know you got a spot to crash whenever out in Long Island.

It's so far.

So far from what? Hollywood asks. *The train is the train.*

You right.

I don't tell him about the screenplay. I just hope *Wings*, the novel, will be better received as we bump around the city toward our destination. Asian Public is a cool restaurant/bar in the worst way. The ID policy allows for a few profitable loopholes, and the crowd is predominantly young New City University students, but you can't beat the prices for food and drink, so well worth it. Accordingly, Asian Public has become our place. At this point it's damn near a ritual. Hollywood and I split a plate of fries and fried calamari.

Be right back. Carry my messenger bag to the bathroom, remembering I haven't brushed my teeth or showered today. I pay attention to myself in the mirror. There always seems to be a faint reddish line across the horizon of my eyes like pink ice around Saturn. I'm pretty sure my eyelids don't close all the way when I sleep, but hard to know. Load a healthy amount of toothpaste and get to scrubbing. There's a pale, inch-long scar above my left eyebrow from when I caught a bottle with my forehead in Atlanta. I spit, rinse, and rub the cut-and-sewn reminder. Hear a knock on the door and someone working at the doorknob. A stranger steps in.

Oh, my bad, he says. *It's cool though, right? I can just go like this.* He approaches and simulates pissing with his back to me.

Not cool, I say.

Why you tripping? He laughs. *It's all good. You been locked up before, right?*

Oh, nah. I pack up and kick off. *You got it.*

The biggest perk to Asian Public is that we've all succumbed to the ritual of it. After a hard day's work or a long stretch of boredom, you know someone you know is going to be there. What starts off as a classic New City creep show ends up being a decent night. In a stroke of great fortune I manage to sell six copies of *Strays*.

For time's sake I'll do a quick roll call of those present and accounted for in our New City Asian Public gang. Blue and Big, you've met already. Big's lowkey the social glue and discoverer of Asian Public. Blue's super chill and slightly antisocial, so he'll probably be leaving soon. Lamb, the young lady by the bar with the green hobbit jacket and the smile, works in fashion. She's from Jersey. I don't know why we call her Lamb except it's short for Lamb Chop and she told us when we first met years ago not to call her Lamb. Q., the well-heeled young lady in orange, is one of my first collectors. We've known Q. since twelve or so as well. Buddy next to her I'm not sure about, but he never stops talking. Charming dude with the baldy and the nose ring is Solo. He used to work with Hollywood and me at New City Public. Next to him is Raji, a young rapper who went to church with Big and Blue as kids. The two trees next to Lamb are my brothers from boarding school, A.K. and A.U. The two bearded professionals hovering over their miso soups are Soony and Nikko. The tall Cali girl is Row, whom you've already met. We went to undergrad and played ball together. The flower in the yellow dress and all the hair is Necca, who writes for social media. The stocky politician putting Necca in a headlock is Dez from Buffalo. The two gentlemen by the door are Shep and Marty. Marty you met already I think, and Shep is a boxer/painter from Brooklyn. The both of them are well versed in the fine art of breaking human beings apart but are also supremely creative. That thousand-watt smile next to them is Oski from Jersey, who does a little bit of everything and also owns and manages a boutique on the Lower East Side. The short, sweet Japanese lady walking around with the bowl cut is the owner of Asian Public. She used to own a handful of restaurants in the city, but now it's just the one. And that's it really. You know the folks at the table. Oh, the young man behind the bar is Russ, and the Nordic shuttling out fries and drinks is Codes, both geniuses in their own right. On any given night there's bound to be packs of us ripping and running through the city still trying to touch it all, so it's nice to have a depot with familiar faces.

Did you know . . . I tap Blue, my favorite random conversationalist. *Did you know the earth accumulates tons of stardust from asteroids and whatnot every day? Did you know that our dead skin cells, which is stardust, is mostly what we call dust today?*

Sounds good. He's not impressed.

Codes pulls some tables together for us. *The degenerates' last supper.*

Hollywood tells Oski the story of how we hit the crackhead and her front tooth pinging off the windshield.

Did you know . . . , Blue asks me. *Did you know that two-thirds of the New City phone book changes every year?*

Damn. That's a lot of people. I think about it.

That's a lot of security deposits. Blue finishes his ginger ale.

Manager Ron wipes down the windows looking out to the garden. Moving out of Murkt Street brought me back to our celestial origins as I uncovered all the glorious detritus that somehow found its way under beds or on boxes, and the army of windows of 1497 Murkt Street.

Blue kicks off as expected. Big, Hollywood, and I roll back to Gold Street. In classic form we manage to get yelled at by Mom Dukes for being too loud. The whole night feels retro and makes sense, since Gold Street is where it all started. It was the summer before Saint Timothy when Mom and Pop Dukes allowed Big and me to live on our own on Gold Street so long as we both got jobs. So began my adult dance with New City. I tackle some laundry, shower, change into a fresh V-neck, iron the wrinkles out my new shirt, and watch on as the brothers play video games. It's a near perfect weekend.

Monday comes around and I find myself on another couch not my own. I kneel before it and say a prayer. I brush teeth, pack bag, and step out into the cold.

12 / BLAZE

THE GYM ON THE TENTH FLOOR AT NEW CITY PUBLIC
is a padded cage. The walls are lined from ground to goal in pro-
tective blue padding, and the rest up to the lights is cage. What's
being protected from what you'll have to judge. Before we get too
psychological, let's do some math. Gym is a non-core class. Core
classes (math, science, humanities, etc.) are taught in sections of no
more than thirty kids. Non-core classes (gym, dance, drama, etc.)
are taught in double sections of up to sixty kids. One teacher plus
sixty kids times multiple balls in air at various times equals chaos.
For most subs gym class is hell. It's a completely unstructured en-
vironment with twice the personalities and elevated hormones. To
me, it's a world I don't mind. The padding is cut and slashed with
yellow foam scars. The blue nylon thread holds the scars together
like stitches.

I put my chair by the front door so no one sneaks in or out and
open my paper. Reading between the lines of what's considered
newsworthy material and watching over a mass of students too
large to properly watch over, I'm struck by a new thought and a
memory. There are a million thoughts running through my mind,

but two land with authority. I walk to the window and take in the city. I get the sense that freedom is more than an actual experience. Being stuck at work doesn't feel too liberating, but it's an investment into freedom in the future, and I can be far less free than this moment. Freedom seems to be a state of mind. The second thought I have after a volleyball blasts the pad next to me is a memory. I remember Nana reading her paper as I'm sitting and reading. Nana used to force my best friend Timothy, my cousin Michael, and me to read our books while she read the paper. I loved being outside catching snakes and jumping off hills, so it was a struggle for me. I remember Timothy seemed to enjoy the structure. I remember Michael doing everything he could not to read. It's so real, it's like we're kids again—until I recall they're both no longer here. A soccer ball blasts the blue door. I realize it's just me sitting here watching strangers' kids.

Can we go to the bathroom? a pair of gigglers ask.

No. I don't look up.

No? Why not?

No because "we" like to hang out in the stairwell.

A volleyball screams by my face. There are only so many ways a kicked ball can travel, and I'm watching out for that.

I said! I turn the page. *Do* not *kick the volleyballs!*

Please can we go?

I check my phone. *It's five minutes left. One at a time or hold it. Matter of fact.* I reach up and flick the lights twice. *Class over! I'm not writing no notes for next period, so hustle up. Plenty of time.*

Students are always hesitant to go back to the reality of core classes. I feel their pain. The fantasy of freedom melts quick. Gym clears out. I figured I'd be hot in my new button-down, but it's surprisingly comfortable. Walk up to a napper in the corner and nudge him. *Wake up. Class is done.* Nothing happens. Nudge him harder. No movement. *Yooo. Wake up!* I kneel and shake him by the shoulders how they teach in first-aid class. I can't even give light to the scary ideas bumping my right brain as I see no response. Luckily napper opens his eyes. *Class is over,* I tell him. *Hop to.*

He stands, shoulders his backpack, and stumbles off. My phone buzzes. Text from Maggy saying she doesn't need me to sub tomorrow. Buzzsaws, hammers, and all types of construction sounds start back up above head. Check my bank account and see red negative numbers. Revisit the last transaction, which overdrafts me. Doesn't make sense until I go back a few more transactions. As the students had to return to their core classes, I too have to descend back into a city I've loved who has yet to love me. Unbutton my top button. Ten years of humble pie has taught me creative ways to disguise my ambition, but I always felt like I'd be king of the world at some point. New City was supposed to be a launch point. Failure is a temporary state I'm sure, but I'm still steeping in it. Slap the blue padding under the goal and hear a thread pop in my shirt. Deep down it feels as if my truth is slowly tearing the facade of humble me apart.

Suit yourself! a construction worker yells from above. Sounds Eastern European.

Suit myself, another replies sarcastically. *You should do comedy!*

Jackhammers. Sit against the padded wall and magic plaster dust falls from the lights. I hope it's not asbestos. I sit and watch this stardust roll in the sunlight and remember the view from my window seat on that would-be flight to Saint Timothy. Worlds apart, but they feel to inhabit the same space today. I remember my view from our house in Saint Timothy and how much peace I felt there. I felt like a king. *How can I feel this*—I stand up and dust my hands off—*and still harbor so much fear?* I thought the questions in life would get easier with acts of bravery, but it seems to me they're landing harder and colder. "Where am I going to sleep tonight?" is not the type of life question you expect to be dealing with. It pops up on its own at random times, such as now, with asbestos raining down. Sometimes it's more casual and informative. Other times, such as today, it's heartbreaking. I get the urge to move out of the way of the asbestos shower and feel utterly alone. I feel desperate, muted, foolish, prideful, and lost. I put on a good face for the students on their way up, but I am neither strong nor stable nor well enough to be telling anybody anything.

A middle school student peeks in and says something about a substitute. Before long there's a flood of eager students ready to drive me nuts. They care little where I'll be sleeping tonight. Nor how far I've drifted. Oh, another perk of substituting non-core classes is getting double duty. Why double? Simple. The high school gym teacher only teaches high school. The middle school gym teacher only teaches middle school. The substitute gym teacher can cover both. Not nice.

Have a seat around the eagle, I say. This is where I gain control. The students are used to pushing teachers around with sheer numbers and making us repeat ourselves to the point of exhaustion. Not me. Not today. I've learned to let the mob have at the marginalized rebellion and make the leaders fight for their freedom. Like clockwork, a student will come up and ask if they can have a ball or what we're doing today or something to separate themselves. This student will almost always be a leader.

Is it open gym time? Red Cap tries to play it cool.

Have a seat around the eagle, I say. *Thank you.* Just to show I'm not evil, I take a wild shot and retrieve the basketball. *I'll wait,* I say.

Yo! Red Cap yells. *Sit down so we can play!*

More and more students come to realize they have to police themselves to play.

What generally happens is some of you do what you're supposed to do. Students begin to sit. *The rest do what you want.* I take a long three from the wing.

Brick! Laughter and chatter.

I'm not going to sit here and tell you which is right or wrong. That's for you to figure out at another time. And right changes from one moment to the next. Three from the top. Cash. *It's crazy that I'm the one who teaches you about right and wrong.* Of all people. *What's right today may be wrong tomorrow. And vice versa. Do you agree or disagree?*

Groans.

I know they're engaged at least. *Who's brave enough to tell me why or why not?* They all start talking. *Raise your hand!* I call on a young lady with black nail polish and a pink not-suitable-for-work crop top. *Miss.*

You said what's right today might be wrong tomorrow. She picks at her cuticles. *But truth doesn't change.*

I stop dribbling. *For those of you who didn't hear that or just now decided to pay attention, the young lady . . . What's your name?*

Winter.

Winter raises an excellent point. She says pure truth never changes. How many of you agree with that?

Shoot a deep three.

You can't hit that again.

Can we play now?

I thought this was open gym?

Come on!

Pure truth, I agree with Winter, *doesn't change. But* the *truth changes all the time. Tell me something that's true.*

We want open gym!

True.

You can't shoot!

Now we know—I take a good look at a shot—*that's not true.* Deep three. Miss bad and the mob goes wild.

The world is round!

Aha! I chase the ball down. *There was a time when if you and I even had this debate we'd be tortured or killed. How's that for truth? Everyone knew the world was flat. Truth. Fact. Period. If you argued it . . .* Slit my throat for dramatic effect.

Winter re-raises hand. *But we know it's true now.*

We know, right? How many of us have been to outer space? How many of us have actually seen the curvature of the earth?

The class laughs.

Well, good morning!

Are you an anarchist? Winter asks.

I don't understand anarchy. I like rules. But that's me. Now . . . rules to the gym. Shoot a midrange. *Anyone needs to use the restroom, get a drink, you have a personal issue, or anything, you ask. If you have to touch a door for any reason, you ask. One at a time. Don't kick the volleyballs or basketballs. I repeat, do not kick the volleyballs or basketballs. No play fighting, wrestling, special moves, or nothing like that. If I have to speak to you twice, if you can't share, or if you can't figure out how to get along, I'm going to get angry. I don't like being angry. Last but not least, don't touch me. I'm a germaphobe and I just bought this nice white shirt.*

Mixed laughter.

Any questions or comments?

Nobody.

Okay. Now, I think I've had all of you before, but for those that don't know me, I'm Mr. Papers. Some people call me Coach, some people call me Mister, some people call me Mr. June, which is fine, but June's my first name. All I ask is that you conduct yourselves like decent human beings and I'll respect you as such. One-time-only deal. Think of a good question, any question, and I'll answer it. So long as it's not crass. Right now. One time only.

Most students are timid and somewhat excited. Some students, like I imagine I would have been, can't wait for moments like this. An actual challenge or a time to ask a great question.

A wide-eyed student with bleach-stained jeans raises his hand. *How much do you make as a substitute?*

Great question. What's your name?

Michael.

Michael, you're either going to be very successful in life or a starving artist like me. That was an excellent question. As a substitute teacher in New City I make one hundred and fifty bucks per day minus taxes. And it goes down the more days I work, so if I clock a full week I get paid about five hundred dollars not the seven hundred and fifty you might imagine.

That's, like, not good, he says. *That's . . . minimum wage.*

Facts. And I have a master's degree. Distribute the balls as democratically as I can imagine, throw a few long, hand a couple to the quiet students, and let the rest end up where they may. Put my chair back in front of the door and read my paper. A woman tackled the Pope apparently. Off the chain. It's a full-time job figuring out who's what nowadays. Basketball rolls my way and I get roped into hooping with the students.

Time out. I stop play. OG time-out. *Why y'all keep shooting threes?*

Shrugs.

This is twenty-one. Threes and twos all count for two. Three is just a longer, harder shot. Makes no sense.

We like a challenge, one says.

You not trying to win, I offer. *All that energy and you playing to lose.*

The rest of the day's confetti. I give a copy of *Strays* to the literacy teacher in the office and kick off. Sun drops as I walk the city. My mood improves from the earlier madness, and I stop in a café to get down the bones of it. I don't know why I felt so immobilized by uncertainty other than the asbestos triggering asthma flashbacks of hospital visits. I feel okay now. Coffee helps. The sun paints West Fourth brick red as it retires. I get a text from Ma with the picture of kindergarten me cheesing hard in my yellow blazer and gray tie. Quite the outfit for a five- or six-year-old. I had asthma bad then. More than once I was taken to the hospital to get pumped with steroids. The toughest part for me was telling Nana or Ma I couldn't breathe. I would always wait until the very last minute, when I felt like I was about to die. By then of course everyone would be mad for other reasons. Why wait? I never wanted to be a burden to anyone. I was always hyperaware of my own weight. Life was hard enough for everyone as it was. Every once in a while, more often than I'd like to admit, I decide to steal something as a middle finger to the invisible hands keeping good people down while psycho rich people get richer. Today I decide I'm stealing a blazer.

I'm walking down Sixth with some clue where I'm going and take a sharp right once I find Men's Styleshop. A muted door chime rings behind me. Tall statue of a security guard stares. *Can he read my mind?* I wonder to myself.

Clerk sizes me up. *Thirty-four long. Sixteen collar.*

I nod, surprised. Great. Suit shop full of telepaths.

I'm overqualified. He stands from his computer desk and ties his dreads up.

My mother brought me to the Bronx a few times when I was a kid. She took me shopping with her. I found out later that our fantastic little shopping trips tended to net more goods than we had money for. I began stealing myself when I was younger because things are cheaper when you don't pay for them. It's a good way to save. Excitement turns to confusion and my logistical nightmare. I expected way more cover. It's basically me, the two employees, and my stomach doing donuts. I try on a blue blazer and damn near run for the restroom. I might have to put this caper on ice. Of all times to have the bubble guts. I notice my face is grimacing and the clerk is looking. *I'm looking for a nice suit.* I feign thought. *Nothing tailored per se. Just a nice fit.*

It's your lucky day, Dread says. *We have a black-tag promo today.* He walks around the counter. *Tailored is always your best bet, though.*

I thumb through the rack until I uncover a waxy black blazer with red silk lining.

Dread checks the size. *Fate.* He smiles. *Let me find you a shirt. French cuff or—*

Just like this. I point to the mannequin. Walk over to the tall mirrors and check my new self.

You might want to take the arms in a tiiiny bit, Dread says. *Maybe not.*

It's perfect, I say, remembering the power of my white button-down. I can already feel the blazer's magic synergizing with the shirt. Cheat codes. Armor in a world of capitalists.

The guard crosses his arms as if he can lowkey read my mind. I don't know if it's the blazer doing work already, but rather than getting more concerned, I start to feel game. Text from Maggy asking me to sub tomorrow after all provides the perfect cover. I pull my phone out like the president is calling.

My love! I answer my imaginary girlfriend's imaginary call and listen, concerned. *I'm picking up the suit for tomorrow,* I say. Find my debit card, all serious in the face. Dread returns with shirt and slacks. *I haven't tried it on yet,* I inform my imaginary girlfriend. *Blazer looks great, though.* I listen reluctantly to some imaginary bad news. *I don't have time for that right now. I wish I could. Huh? I'm about to try on the suit! I'll call you back.*

Dread hands me a ticket. *First booth,* he says.

Step in, lock door, set phone timer alarm for four minutes, dress, step out slowly, and smile in front of the big mirrors. Phone vibrates. Answer to my imaginary girlfriend. *I'm trying the suit on as we speak. I promise.* She's getting her nails done and insists I let her see it. Women. *Where's that?* I shake my head and check the mirror again. *Trust me, it's perfect.* I aim phone receiver to Dread. *How does this suit look?*

It's perfect, he yells.

Risky, but it works.

Alriiiiiight. Disappointed, I unbutton the shirt. *Where you at? Oh, that's right around the corner from here, I think.* Feign fatigue, tell Dread I have to clear it with the boss lady first, and put on a struggle to remove blazer. Sounds and all.

Where you going? he asks. *Nail Spa?*

I think that's it.

Go 'head, man. He waves me off. *You good.*

You sure? I don't want to get you in trouble. I nod to sergeant security over there.

We're open till eleven. Plenty of time.

Up until this point it's a game of appearances. Now it becomes clear to me the clerk is a genuinely nice guy and I'm just a con man. It hurts. Makes me feel I have to return the suit at some point. Maybe. Probably won't, but the feeling is there.

Be riiight back, I say. *Thanks.*

No problem.

The bubble guts return. The loss of virtue, the fear, the abandoned principles, all mix together like a liter of soda inside me. Suddenly, the moment becomes too much and I begin to freeze up. I shoulder my bag, but my feet won't move. And my legs feel like jelly. Force a smile but still nothing. Desperate for action of any kind, I commit to leaning forward. Either I will face-plant or I will pop the clutch. It works. Feet do what feet are supposed to do. Sergeant security steps aside. *Ink pack?* I ask him.

Nah, you good. He waves me out. Even he sounds like a nice guy.

I exit and zigzag for a dozen or so blocks just to be sure no one's following me. Coast clear, I power walk the city and approach that big black box sculpture drunks love to spin at Astro Place. I've walked by it hundreds if not thousands of times and never touched it. Walk up and push until it spins. I keep walking toward NoHo. In a strange twist of fate I end up in front of the gallery from my first day in the wind, when the winds were ferocious and I was scared to step out. There's an art-show party going on inside. I wonder if there's anyone in the gallery about to step out into the unknown as I was. I doubt it, but I look anyway. Feels like a lifetime ago I considered myself an artist. I carry on toward the action and walk among crowds, amused at how people step out of the way for me. As a young Black man, I might as well be Moses parting the Red Sea. Sidewalk traffic that would normally pinball me into oblivion suddenly splits like schools of fish. To my youngest readers who haven't had to deal with the sticky sides of human nature, this is like your parents waking you up on the first day of school and saying never mind this whole school thing. Today we're doin' whatever you want. I raise my hand for a cab and step out to the curb. Cabbie pulls up and rolls down his window. *Where you headed?*

You stopped! I laugh.

Uptown?

Why not? I open the door and hear a yell from across the street. *You stopped first try.*

Juuuneeey!

Hear my name again and see Hollywood with shopping bags and a friend. Exit the cab and cross the street.

Hollywood laughs so hard he has to hold his stomach. *Now I know you a federal informant,* he says.

Daps.

Ebony. He introduces the young lady with a red bandana like Tupac. *This my godbrother Junie, aka Donnie Tabasco. Watch what you say around him.* He slaps me in the chest and, with a big smile, checks the inside of the blazer for a wire.

Ebony's confused.

You around this weekend? he asks, suddenly serious.

I am, I say.

If you still need that bread for Nana, I got the best play since pants with pockets. Your driver's license is good, right?

It is.

Ebony uncle wanted me to wheel his whip to the Cape. Four hundred clean . . .

Translation: Ebony's uncle wants Hollywood to drive (wheel) his automobile (whip) to Cape Cod (the Cape). In exchange for said labor, he'll pay $400, and it's legal (clean).

Plus gas. I told him I'd do it, but I gotta do daddy duty this weekend. I been buggin'.

You see, Ebony . . . I try to find the words. *When things sound too good to be true*—sniff Hollywood—*but smell a little fishy, chances are it's a setup.*

Not this time. She smiles.

It's her uncle's whip. Hollywood looks at me like I'm stupid. *Take this walk with us. We going to Oski's real quick.*

Cool. I button my top button. *I was floating anyways.*

Gathering information? Ebony guesses.

High fives.

We walk and take in the city anew. Nights like tonight remind me why I fell in love with New City in the first place.

SCHOOL

1 / LABOR

I WORRY A LOT, I'M NOW REALIZING. I WORRY ABOUT many things and quite often. The realization reminds me of a short story I read in an elevator on my way to English class a few years back about a drifter rummaging through dusty toys in an abandoned house. The drifter realizes at some point how permanent the idea of home must have felt to the family and how fleeting permanence really is. I feel the same about my recent worries now as if I can see clearly that the fears, thoughts, and ideas are all just habits that have no more truth or permanence than whatever I choose to assign them. Finessing the jacket and going against my own principles allowed me to recognize how much of a worrier I was. I worry about opinions, spatial awareness, history, repercussions, tone of voice, principles, right versus wrong, and whatever millionth layer of society I happen to be on. I know where it comes from. Some concern is very important. The lion's share of the worry is not only pointless but also corrosive and counterproductive. I'm worried about making mistakes and making the same mistake twice. I'm worried I may be misunderstood and trying at every turn to be clear. I'm worried I'll be labeled this or that and worrying about karma. It's so much. It's ridiculous. I'm a substitute teacher. This blazer is my self-induced reality check. It opens me back up to the world again and clears my closet of the self-righteousness trophies I'd been subconsciously collecting. The act of stealing's humbling in a powerful way. Humanizing. Of course, as soon as I come to some resolution about the deed, I feel regret. I remember how it felt to lie to that young man who was just doing his job. A new fear paves the way for a slight panic. Fears. Second thoughts. I take a deep breath and face reality.

Hold up. Hollywood stops us and tells Ebony we'll catch up. *Let me get you that sixty I owe you.*

We walk into bank.

Before I forget.

I assume we're ditching Ebony until we actually stand on line. There's a couple ahead of us, and ahead of them an older gentleman with a Korean War cap. I keep my post office nightmare memory to myself. Maybe it's me, but old people don't seem that old anymore. To watch this guy move, you'd think he was thirty. Maybe I never properly respected geriatric athleticism. Look out the wall of window and see Ebony talking to a young lady on the corner. Recognize her face.

Who's that Ebony's talking to? I ask Hollywood.

No clue. I'm tempted to go find out, but this cash is critical. Hollywood turns away from the teller with cash in hand, I remember not to worry so much, and everything goes slow motion for me. My spidey senses are on a thousand, and I can't tell if it's jacket magic or no-worry vibes, but I feel like a superhero. The young couple, the tellers, and Hollywood all slow to a glacial pace. I realize that I too am stuck physically in slow motion but my perception is still normal speed, and I peep that the surprisingly agile vet is actually robbing the bank. Hollywood's grabbing an empty envelope as the vet's making a hasty exit, and they collide.

Yiiiiikes, Hollywood says, unsure of how or why, and time returns to normal speed.

The vet wobbles and drops a stack of cash. Hollywood's eyes bug out. The vet scoops his money and dips. Soon as the vet hits corner news spreads and bank folks start yelling and crying into cell phones. Hollywood and I slide off before the cops come and make a long day longer.

I can't believe the bank got hit up. Hollywood laughs. *By an old head.*

Ebony's nowhere to be found, so we head to Oski's.

We need to write a movie, Hollywood says again, tired of saying it.

You been saying that.

Exactly. How's the screenplay going?

Trashed for now, I confess. *I was trying to do too much.*

Story of my life. Hollywood spit shines his golden loafer. *It couldna been that bad, though.*

I had Somali pirates in the Mediterranean, I tell him.

Sounds feasible to me.

And magic boxes that talk to people.

Yikes.

We walk in brisk New City winds. Hollywood does the sidewalk tango with a pair of photo-snapping tourists, one white, one Black.

It's bugged out how much a suit changes behavior. I feel like the president. I smile and sneak a photo of the photographers shooting a hand-painted FaceCrook ad.

You! a Black Jew yells at the poor tourists, who know neither the nature of his predicament nor the venom in the bush. *You are the ones who want to enslave, you swine!*

You have no clue what you're talking about, White Tourist retorts. *You don't know me.*

They're just loud and obnoxious, Black Friend says.

How is it that this grown Black man, Black Jew asks, chuckling, *sounds like a white girl?*

You're the racist! White Tourist says. *Look at you!*

Let me educate you, you snake. If it wasn't for your skin, I'd swear you were a white man. You dress like a European, you speak and think American, and you carry yourself like a white man. Where's your pride? Your history? You have no knowledge of self. Cowards like you disgust me. Swine. Proverbs! He taps a disciple who's been waiting, Bible in hand. *Book twenty-eight, verse one, please!*

Disciple snaps to. *"The wicked flee when no one pursues, but the righteous are bold as a lion. When a land transgresses, it has many rulers, but with a man of understanding and knowledge, its stability will long continue."*

Many rulers! Black Jew reiterates. *You follow false idols. False prophets. You know who we follow? God. You know who we fear? No one. Thank you, God.*

Black Friend laughs. *You know absolutely nothing about me.*

Fear. The Black Jew crosses that invisible line an inch or two from face. *Look at you. So scary you prolly afraid to admit it.* He sniffs around. *I could smell the fear in you before you turned the corner, snake.*

Let's get out of here. White Tourist pulls his friend away. *We're on vacation, and these guys are obviously nuts.*

Proverbs, please!

Aight, my guy. Hollywood kicks off.

I try to figure out what to do with my new self. University library is closed. I end up at McDowell's. Two scribes are already occupying primo real estate. One scribe has a notebook out, and the other's reading the paper. New City scribes are so literate. I get up to six Mississippi with no idea why I'm counting Mississippis. It happens now and again, I don't know why. It strikes me that it's not even dinnertime yet.

Sir, I hear. *Are you okay?*

I wake up.

Are you okay?

Was I sleeping? I smile, stretch, and stand. *Thanks.*

She smiles and walks back through the employees-only door. I look around and suddenly feel super lonely. Stretch makes me dizzy. No scribes, no drifters, and all the employees are in the back. I'm stuck wondering where everyone went and why my vision is twinkling with those between-dream orbs again. Feels too lonely, so I walk to Asian Public before they close and have myself a few gingers with Codes. Stumble out and hit the train. See two out-of-town scribes in a panhandling battle. One has a guitar, and the other's covered in handmade signs with strange sayings. MY NAME'S JOHN Z LOVETT JR. KIDNAP AN A CUMPUTER MACHINE WAS PUT IN MY BRAIN. THESE EVIL WICKED BASTARDS SHOULD BE SEARCH OUT SEIZED AND PUT IN PRISON FOR THEIR . . . Can't see the rest. They're laminated light explosives. I'm listening to music, so I can't hear much of the battle besides guttural noises and makeshift explosions. Open my eyes and both bums are gone. Scribes I should say. No more bums.

Scribes from now on. It's not their lack of funds that makes them homeless any more than their love of literature. Count doors and stop at seven. Seven is a good number. Hop a few dimensions, and suddenly I'm at the top floor of an eerily familiar mall with a broken escalator and a ladder. My hands are sweaty and I'm afraid. A fall from this floor would be fatal, I think, even in dream state. Climbing down the ladder, I see a kid and his parents. I guess they're waiting to climb down as well. The kid's name is June. *Look, Mommy!* He points to me. *Remember when I was scared to climb the ladder?* She tells him to be nice to me as I feign confidence. Wake up woozy and disappointed. Readjust my bag and lay my head. Me and a gang of wrestlers are locked in a caged death match. The more I try not to fight, the more I'm punished. It's very *Invisible Man*–ish. We're all painted and dressed the part, but I can't see myself. Find a corner and try to hide there, but sound off a coward alarm. Security comes to get me and June, and his parents reappear from the dream before. *Look, Mommy!* he says. *June's not a wrestler.* Mom starts rooting for me. Little June too. It gives me courage. I walk toward the mob of wrestlers and feel a tap on my shoulder.

Sir. I open my eyes. *Keep an eye on that bag. It's a lot of pickpockets out this time of night.*

Thanks. Cop nods and keeps on. Cross my arms and put my head back down. Decide to get some water as soon as possible as soon as I wake up. Big's speeding in reverse down a hectic Brooklyn side street. We skid to a stop, and he hops out and disappears. I step out into the middle of a firefight between firemen and Muslims. I'm on the fireman side of the street, which in a firefight is all the sidedness you need. Make my way to the firehouse, and a fireman turns his pistol to me. He fires and I'm like Neo in the matrix, only slower, and the bullets stick to my shirt. Hustle out of harm's way and catch a couple more slugs. Legs grow weak. Realize I'm dreaming again and get a second wind. Bent on survival I squeeze water out the bullet holes and by nightfall I forget about the flesh. Shooting stops, but it's all too quiet to be over. Creep around and run into a caravan of black Suburbans. A bunch of black suits hop out, so I fall in line and follow them to a warehouse where we approach the president of the United States.

Sir! Sir! I lay my life story on him. I tell the president how I got shot and plead my case that I have all the potential in the world, just no cosign. The president has a brief conversation with some of his advisers, looks me in the eye, and says, *Okay.* I wake up feeling like a million bucks, only to see a train full of people going to work far too early and remember I'm a hundred thousand dollars in debt with some vivid dreams. I feel sick and super thirsty, like I'm dehydrated. There's room for another person to sit next to me if I move over, but I don't. Skin cold-sweating and stomach twisting, I transfer and hop off at Wall Street. Pass two newlyweds kissing at city hall for some photographers and try to take the shot myself as my phone dies. Find myself on cobblestone streets again standing before the African slave memorial I always randomly stand before. Last time was when I was explaining my felonious adventures at the board of education. Every time I see this slave memorial gravesite on this back block I only find when I'm lost, I feel a great sense of shame and amazement. I'm ashamed so many people went through so much for me to be here and I'm not always grateful. I'm amazed how memory does and does not work. This cobblestone street I'm standing on was built by African slaves. Broadway and

much of Wall Street and New City were built by my ancestors under the threat of death. The cobblestone, the skyscraper reaching
out toward heaven, the grids, and the guts and bones of New City
were built by historical forces so brutal that there's little effort to
revisit. Hell, if I wasn't lost again on this back block I only find
when I'm spun around, I wouldn't remember. Hidden here in plain
sight and flanked by federal and city municipalities is a burial—
actually buried here are the bones of nameless ancestors who built
without knowing the strange routes it'd take to one day bring a
long-lost historian home. I take note in my journal and keep it
moving. Walk into first light and end up at New City University.
Pretend I'm with a study group and sneak into the stacks. Find the
fountain and hydrate. Elevator up to the top floor and try to shake
this nervousness I feel. Lay my head.

Sorry. A young lady wakes me. *Can I borrow your charger?*

My phone just died, I say.

No worries. She thanks me and sits at a study table. She doesn't
strike me as the type of kid to steal, but who am I to judge? I lay
my head again and the world starts to spin. Stand and hustle to
the bathroom. Drink more water. Return to seat and see young
lady scribing furiously into her notebook. I unplug my charger and
bring it to her.

Thank you so much. She smiles.

Whatchu writing? I ask.

Fiction.

One-word-answer status already, huh? How old are you?

How old do I look?

I'd say a young seventeen.

Sixteen.

That's what's up. You want to be a writer?

I am a writer.

You, ah . . . The spins remix my thoughts. My brain throbs.

Are you okay? she asks.

I'm dehydrated. You, ah . . . Notice a nose ring.

Know what's funny? I feel like whenever I'm hungover or groggy I always end up doing something charitable for somebody. Somehow they're always just there perfectly placed in time and space for me to help. Go take another drink from the fountain. It's wild because helping other people out while I'm struggling is the last thing I want to do. Nevertheless, I walk back to her table, sit down, and assist as best I can. I give her all the wisdom and intuitive advice I can muster up from my quarter-million-dollar hobo mind. I'm talking a full-on life dump here. Poor kid.

2 / DEPTH

BIG, BLUE, AND HOLLYWOOD ARE WATCHING A SUR-
vival show at Q.'s in Stytown. Thankful I'm feeling much better, I
head over. These two professional survivors (and film crew) strand
themselves on an island and document their struggle. First thing
they need is fire. Fatherly-looking guy fails and goes looking for
protein. Motherly-looking one, barefoot with a bandana, works
at two pieces of bamboo. Reminds me of the young lady from the
library starting her journey on the path to discovery. The patience
it will take, the respect for process, the diligence—all the work
from smoke to spark to ember to fire. I say a quick prayer for her. I
pray that she stays strong and has the courage to uncover her own
truth. I pray she anticipates a brilliant success so that it's worth
every struggle. I say a prayer for everyone I can think of, including
myself. I pray for us all. I pray, I pray, and I pray. From the outside
looking in I'm just watching television. That's why journaling's so
important. It's another camera. It'll be corrupted with a lot of your
own slants, but alas you'll be able to see them. After a word or two
it's all fiction. All that really matters is the living—that you opened
yourself up to the full possibility of experience.

3 / KEYS

A FEW MORE OF Q.'S FRIENDS COME OVER. WE TALK art and politics, party, and it transforms into the most comfortable couch-pillows-on-the-floor crash ever. After all's said and done, you have to find the spark in yourself. Read books of interest and value. Read more. Don't spend too much time talking about other people, take care of your family, and tend to your own fire. By the time you read these words, your formal education will be either severely devalued or rigid and inapplicable. If you were paying attention you'd know you're supposed to be learning how to learn, which is an endless pursuit. Your vote or the democratic voice people died for you to have can be powerful or nothing more than a meal ticket for the savage you least expect. Inevitably, you will still have to feed yourself. Don't be fooled, dear future leaders. You have to figure out what you want and work for mastery until you succeed. People waste years talking gossip, politics, race, sex, religion, nationality, culture, pride, identity, and so on, while the true value of their time and effort is hidden in plain sight. Fear under the clever guise of control or protection is quantified, packaged, sold, distributed, and redistributed with little to no value for the user. People've been plotting for years on how to properly eat your lunch under the cover of night. If you think they'll simultaneously be tending to your spark too, you might as well toss *Wings* out the window and watch to see if it catches fire and flies away like a phoenix.

Wake up like a ninja and step out refreshed into another New City morning. A rowdy pack of students cut across the park, and I feel for their loss of innocence already. I remember and I pray for them.

Yo, one says to his friends. *Watch out so the man can get through.*

I appreciate that. I thank him.

Ain't nothing, bro.

Approach the edge of the park and realize I'm power walking nowhere. Stop and turn around. Sometimes I get fired up and just keep going. Also I have spazzes. Too much energy. You can only write for so long. Look for leniency in the park and run into Row.

June! What's poppin', B?

I can't call it, I tell her. *How you?*

Super late.

Handle your biz.

We hug and she kicks off.

I'm getting free tickets to Lincoln tonight if you're not doing anything.

My eyes light up and I nod yes.

Cool. I'll hit you.

Row hurries off and I drift until I wash ashore on a Times Square back block. Approach a vested tourist straining to position her family perfectly in front Ram's Head Hotel for a photo.

Walk past and stand for a moment under the golden ram above the entrance.

Heads up, chief, voice behind me says. Faux-casual-looking suit hops out a midnight-blue Lamborghini, opens the door for his lady friend, and lobs the keys to me. The Lamborghini keys are crossing the sky and I'm realizing he thinks I'm the valet and the happy tourist family is leaving with their picture from in front of the Ram's Head Hotel. Suit overcooks the toss, but we stretch out and make the catch. Seam in shirt pops.

S'poooosed to raaaaain? Slow-motion effect on the voice. He thought we were looking at the sky possibly when we were admiring the golden ram and is now asking if it's supposed to rain.

No rain today, I assure him.

He smiles and hands me a twenty-dollar bill. *Keep her up front if you can,* he whispers.

You got it. I jog around to the driver side as I imagine a valet would, hop in, and consider my options. In this precise moment I don't want to be opportunistic or dishonest, but I also don't want to be a hypocrite. I remember Dinhead County Jail and how fun that was. I recall a lot here, but my general feeling is I don't care. What are the odds that I'd be so lucky regardless of how it came to be? Who am I to judge really?

4 / CRUISE

I put the Lamborghini in first and pretend I
know where I'm going and what I'm doing. I damn near convince
myself. All the little voices get reduced to an impulse to do exactly
what they tell me not to. I keep going, my faith and I in the wind.
Through the curves and turns I feel the wings of everyone who's
ever dreamed bigger than what life allowed. Speed's another one of
those drugs. I catch a red light. Speed sells itself. A cherry Ferrari
pulls up and revs twice. Three times. There's a good amount of
FDR up ahead, which he's free to have. *It's not mine,* I yell. Throws
me the peace sign. Patrol car pulls up. The old fear is there, but it
doesn't stick. I can't identify with it. Almost as soon as I see the officers looking, I notice their curiosity turning to envy. It's a subtle
but clear moment, and in it I shift quickly from suspect to anom-
aly. I nod and they both nod back twice like a glitch in the matrix.
The jacket was stealing. Peel off. I already did my feeling bad about
that. This is a come-up. Completely different. Third. Wheel past
a Stytown super picking up trash outside. We could have let fear
take us where it may, given the keys back, and imagined what
could have been. We could have retold it as a good story in a good

karma play. We could have listened to logic. We could have enter-tained any one of those thousand little voices telling us the same thing in different languages over and over. We did not. We became rogue. We certainly did not pretend to claim ownership ourselves. For that brief gentle moment, we became one without odds. Wheel Lamborghini back into the parking lot with far less fear than I expected. Park up front. Take keys to the lobby.

Keys. I give keys to clerk. *The blue Lamborghini. He said to keep her up front if you could.*

Confusion. *Looks black, right? Nope. Midnight blue.*

Light jog. I'm watching stardust settle into the lights of Broad-way when my phone vibrates.

Message from Row. *8:45 p.m. show. Meet me there? Leaving Brooklyn now. Should be in city by 8:30 p.m.*

Text back, *Dope.*

5 / SPIT

HAND OUR TICKETS TO THE USHER, WHO SEATS US
five rows from the stage.

I hope we're not in range, I say. *Heard these guys do a lot of spit-*
ting. I unfold the program and test it as a shield.

Row laughs and Broadway folks look like they've never heard a
laugh out loud before.

Tough crowd. We shrug it off.

Sad. Row's disgusted. *Did I see you driving a blue sports car*
today?

I laugh. *Have we met?*

I thought I was tripping. She sits up and looks around.

What's good?

I still have time to get snacks, right?

Definitely.

Row returns with two waters, pretzels, and a pack of licorice.
You don't even want to know how much this was. She laughs.

Eighteen ninety-three?

How'd you know?

Broke and homeless now, I've developed an uncanny sensitivity to pricing. *I'm good at guessing.*

Lights dim and crowd settles into silence. Lights up on actor sporting a long black blazer and a sad face.

Hey, I whisper. *He was on your TV the other night. The night you gave us the box of movies.*

You don't know J.R.? She smirks, confused.

Junior Reid is his full name. He steps forward in silence, spotlight bright, and sings.

You've been called upon the field this evening
You've been all in all this strayed from my heart . . .

Never having seen a major production up close and personal, I figure they could have put a hat on a frog and impressed me. My thoughts? This guy made a hundred million dollars last year, and he's up here on Broadway singing in a dress.

After the show we go back to Row's place and talk it out. She isn't the biggest fan either.

I'm just tired of the persecuted artist's story, she says. *Man up.*

You're going to love my novel, I say.

I still want to read Strays.

I hand her a copy out my messenger and she tries to pay, but I tell her her money's no good. *I still owe you.*

Row walks to fridge. *Every time I see you you're writing,* she says.

I have a tricky memory. I hit the bathroom. *It's nice to be able to revisit things clearly and see how I'm living.* I don't know if I'm relieved or embarrassed she doesn't even ask if I'm staying the night, but I do know I'm at the mercy of kindness, honesty, and hospitality and it is a blessing nonetheless. I have warmth, peace, and solitude. Feels better borrowed sometimes. More graceful. I dry my hands and look up the lyrics from buddy's song.

> *You've been called upon the field this evening*
> *You've been all in all this strayed from my heart*
> *Is this all a part of feeling feelings*
> *This is pain for loving you*
> *With this hardened heart we leave you freedom*
> *When I'm dead and gone will they pray for my soul*
> *And when all the golden memories are taken*
> *Will you care to see if I'm even breathin'*

Apparently, it's about a young poet who's figured out his lover's a spy/traitor. I gathered none of that from what we saw. I think it's one of those things you have to know about beforehand to understand. Try to power down for the night and hear keys jingling outside. Pick up shoe and jump into the bathroom. Front door opens. Row steps out. Ricky buckles in her arms.

I'm just so tired, Ricky sobs. *Oh God!* She sees me. *I'm sorry I didn't know you had—*

Please don't be, I say, pretending I have some place to be.

I pack up and kick off. A sanitation truck whips up street dust. A fortunate rat lucks up on a croissant corner. I drift until late. Late late. Still too early for O.J. or any of the other school agents, I circle the block. Seems like every other building has scaffolding. So much change in New City. Black-mesh-covered scaffolding with neon-orange cones and other cautions. New City Public looks like a tall healer offering sage and stray blessings in the predawn blue of New City. Hazard it and try the entrance. Lucky me. Construction workers flow in and out. Elevator up to 11, hit the restroom, and lock the door.

6 / RESPECT

Unpack toiletries and wash up in sink.

Roman shower, I assure myself, lather right pit, and snipe a mosquito-sized airplane out the window leaving ice trails across the sky. Someone knocks. *In here.* Knock again. *In here!* Shave and wash face, power nap in the gym, and substitute Spanish class with seniors. A paper plane floats across a class of two dozen twelfth graders. Look up and lock kind eyes with a student whose arm is still extended.

It was his. He rats on his tablemate.

No interrogation or nothing, huh? I ask. *You just dropping dime.*

Student lowers his head. Chuck does the leave-it-alone face, so I leave it alone. New City Public has a robust special needs population, and it's impossible to know who is what as a substitute other than someone telling you. I thank Chuck for the look and the heads-up. Don, the high school director, pokes his head into the classroom window. Midforties, white ex-teacher type. He steps inside and surprises the class with a visit. Students tighten up.

Wow. I laugh.

Don looks around approvingly and gives the thumbs-up. *Looks like some real learning going on here.*

You should have come in five minutes ago, I tell him.

I can imagine. He laughs.

As soon as Don leaves, the class returns to electronic contraband and celebrity gossip.

Okay. I drop my pencil. *Since no one's doing any Spanish . . . Let me ask you all a serious question.*

I have most of their attention.

Miss with the phone that shouldn't be out. Wait for her to put it away. *Thank you. Now, how many of you have absolutely no idea what you want to be when you grow up?*

A handful of students speak at the same time.

Basic rules to democracy! Everyone is entitled to his or her opinion. If everyone tries to express them at the same time, it makes no difference. Raise your hand, please.

Hands go up.

Thank you. All right. Hands down. Now, let me ask you this. And this is important, so I want you to think about it. As grave as I can be. *If you could have four hundred million or four hundred billion dollars, which would you choose?* I ask this question a lot. It's always interesting to see. Most people lean toward the billions and try to find the catch. Skeptics and religious folks lean toward the millions, and those who do stick by it tight until the tree starts shaking. High schoolers who value respect or are semi-honest get to do whatever. I don't care. Those who try to be slick or disrespectful get weeded out. Chuck's a natural leader, so I more or less let him control things. All I have to do every once in a while is remind him that there's an adult in the room.

7 / LUCK

We walk to Saint Sparks bookshop.

Excuse me. I track down a clerk. *I have a novel here on consignment, and I want to see if anything sold. I see a copy missing, so . . . hoping for the best.*

What's the title?

United Strays of America. *Like stray cats or bullets.*

I'll see if I can help you. Clerk punches numbers into a keyboard. *We don't have it here, but it could be that it sold. Let me check.*

Oh, okay. Thanks.

Any luck? Hollywood asks.

Waiting to see.

No luck. Walk outside and remind myself it's a marathon. Notice a young kid clocking us. He walks over. *'Scuse me.* He looks pitiful. *Would you like to help me and my mother with a donation today? A sandwich, a apple, or any change would be greatly appreciated.*

Pretty sure it's a scam and sad to see kids manipulated like this, but I fish out a single. Ma's pacing back and forth under a rare New City tree.

That's your mother? Hollywood can't help but ask.

Kid feigns confusion. *Yes. That's my mom.*

Is she okay? I can't not ask.

She got motorboat cirrhosis, he says.

8 / ROAD

THE NEXT WEEK, THE MORNING TRAIN'S STUFFED with resigned, dark-eyed people. Sad, sad scene. Walk toward the front and pass a normal-looking platform scribe on a blanket selling toiletries. Normal-looking scribes trip me out. Of all things to look like, they look normal. It's bugged out. I hop on train and head back to my alma mater to get some words in. Luck up on some freelance graphic design work from a New City alum I hoop with. Train downtown for a dollar slice and uptown to link with Hollywood. Nothing like an all-day pass to remind me of how much I love it uptown. Hollywood and I scoop his daughter, Zen, from the babysitter and train back to New City Public.

Before I forget . . . Hollywood texts me Ebony's cousin's phone number. *To pick up the car.*

It's an automatic? I ask.

I assume so.

No more clean V-necks in the supply closet, I train back to Gold Street to get some laundry in before I kick off. Big and Blue play video games, and I lose track of time looking through my old basement stash. Every time I'm about to leave for the Vineyard—where I'm headed after I drop the car on the Cape—I feel a strange, suspended relief. I've become accustomed to letting the Island life surprise me, so I kind of ignore it, but it's clearly there. I'll be rushing to catch a train to a bus or a boat or something, and it will inevitably hit me.

Blue opens the basement door. *It's about that time,* he says.

Bet. Grab bag, daps and hugs, and step out.

Tell Nana we said what's up. Big smiles.

Will do. I'll be back in a couple.

Yessir.

Big locks the locks and heads back inside. It's the transition, I realize on my walk toward the train. It's a tough one. Big had to lock four locks going back inside, for example. On the Vineyard you lock nothing.

Yeeer! Blue yells down Stuyvesant. *You going to Port Authority?*

Yessir.

He unlocks the wheels and pulls up. Every time I leave the city for the Vineyard, I feel a battle for home playing out in real time as I watch the city pass. Streetlights scan the cars as I remember I'm from neither place. I brace myself with a hand on the dash as Blue wheels around an urban jogger.

Any parks on your side? he asks as we hit the thick of Times Square. Black Leggings and Neon Running Shoes almost gets hit. They wait. Blue guns it through two cabbies. *I guess I'm talking to myself here.* He laughs.

No. Here is fine, I tell him. *My bad.*

You sure?

Yessir.

Blue pulls up by a new dollar pizza spot. *Have a safe trip. Hit us when you touch down.*

Will do.

Aight, kid.

One.

Bus terminals and airports. My homes away from homes. Cop my ticket and board in time to find a seat with no seatmate. Sleep like a baby.

Bus driver wakes me. *We're here.*

Where's that?

South Street. Find my bearings, exit to the parking lot, and meet Ebony's cousin with the orange cap.

9 / TIME

JUNE? EBONY'S COUSIN HOPS OUT AND REMOVES HIS orange skully.

He looks familiar.

Buddy said two things to know. He points to the lone car in the lot across the street and daps me. *One, bring receipts for gas.* He laughs. *Two, the trunk stays locked for whatever reason.*

Ebony's cousin tosses me a rabbit-foot keychain.

Sorry, he apologizes. *I'm late for my daughter's basketball game.*

Shrug it off. *Good luck!*

Thanks. Happy Thanksgiving!

You too. I wonder if it's really Thanksgiving. Remind myself to check. Realize this is not a normal thought process at all. I walk to the maroon sedan with the cranberry seats and wait for the tactical team takedown. No movement anywhere, I hop in and smell straight ocean. *Well.* Set mirrors and fasten seat belt. *It's me and you for a bit.* Stash my cash. Minus two ferry tickets and monies for food and drinks, I have $1,206. Even if buddy tries to finesse me off gas, I'm good. Deep breath. Key the ignition and she starts right up. Let her run for a bit. Right onto Church Street. Pull into gas station. Lady in sun hat is on the expensive stuff. Hope she leaves her receipt in the print tray—and jackpot. $52.98. Fill up on that low grade and scan the dark for Interstate signage. Bingo. Buildings recede, turns straighten, and trees become forest again. Driving simplifies to a steadiness of so many miles and so many miles per hour, yet we're barely moving at all. Reminds me of that damn post office line and the vet with his trophy. I wonder if his grandson ever got his gift. Reminds me of the moon and the stars and the speed of our galaxy. I say a little prayer.

10 / FEAR

I've been terrified of cars. I've been haunted by all the heavy vehicular truths hiding behind the illusions of control. A sudden change or a nut on a motorbike reminds me of the accidents I've been in, and for some reason or another I've been in quite a few. When I drive, anything smaller than a deer is a speed bump. I don't lose sight of the fact that we're in a two-ton death trap. No sense in swerving and inviting mayhem. Every twenty or thirty miles there's a small cluster of bright lights and cones closing off the far lane. Men in yellow helmets standing around saw blades six feet tall. Traffic slows because people are nosy and notice a crew of women. Time and a half probably. Somehow there's always infrastructure roadwork to be done during the holidays.

11 / LAWS

THE PACK SPEEDS BACK UP. WE DON'T KNOW EACH other or speak, but we're bound by intuitive adventures in this strange limbo of everywhere and nowhere. *This's how people die*, I say to myself getting deep going eighty. *Kill it, Einstein.* Turn the radio on and try to find something not to listen to. See a light flicker and think I'm having a déjà vu. Déjà vu? Nope. Cop lights. Not sure how long they been behind me. *I'm being pulled over.* I say it to myself to make sure it's not a dream. Pull into a rest stop. Cop walks up to my window as I struggle to roll it down.

License and registration, please. Pop the glove box and pray.

Here you go. Hand documents over.

Cop walks back to his car. I start to revisit my history in a not-so-flattering filter. Large chunks of life pop up on the horizon like icebergs.

You know why I pulled you over?

Wakes me out my paranoid trip. Gums and baby teeth. Looks like he's from Canada or Maine.

I don't, I tell him. Hope he doesn't ask me to get out.

You were doing over seventy.

Try to look as earnest as possible. *I thought I saw sixty-five.*

It's been fifty-five for miles and miles.

Best I can do is grimace.

Due to all the roadwork.

I slowed down. I didn't notice the signs change, I say. *Did they?*

Did they? Yes. Yes, they did. He kicks the rear tire. *You riding a little low, ain'tcha? What's in the trunk?*

Nothing out of the ordinary. I basically incriminate myself.

You won't mind if I have a look, then?

Is that necessary? At this point I might as well arrest and convict myself.

Honestly, it'd just make things easier.

I try a number of pushes and pulls to avoid the inevitable. Cops never go against their hunches.

I try one last shot at collegiate (privileged yet informed). *Officer, unless you have a reason to check my trunk other than misplaced curiosity, I can't let it happen. I'm sorry.*

His head nearly explodes.

In all honesty, if it would get me out of the ticket, I'd show you the trunk, no problem, but it's not just my rights you'd be violating. Buys me more time. *I know it seems strange, but I'm a responsible driver. I just didn't see the signs change. I know I can't be the only one this has happened to.*

You got a Massachusetts license. He flicks it. *Connecticut plates. In Rhode Island. And you're on your way to the Cape?*

I am. I'm basically begging at this point. *If I was going to lie, the story'd be way less complicated than this.*

I see him weighing his logic against his gut, which is a good sign. Cops rarely weigh their logic in front of you unless they're reasonable. Reid is his last name. Officer Reid.

Officer Reid smirks in disbelief.

If you want to give me a ticket, that's fine. I did miss the signs. I know you have to deal with some real nuts out here, so I understand completely.

A drunk ran an elderly woman off the road this morning, he tells me. *She crashed in the marshlands. You have to pay attention on these roads.*

You can tell he's tired of telling people the same thing.

Especially the highway. Officer Reid lets me off with a warning.

Thank you, sir. I start her back up.

He nods. *Be safe.*

I will. I open my messenger bag. *It's my novel.* I show and hand him a copy. *Happy holidays.*

You wrote this? He flips through.

I did.

That's great. He scratches his chin. *Roman numerals!* He belly laughs. *My father's a poet. Cousin's a famous actor.*

And on that note, I wave and pull off.

The road gives time to think. Real time. Hours of uninterrupted space. Separated from the pack and blessed up, I do the speed limit. I feel real peace. I vibe with the hum of rubber and good aerodynamics. I let it be for as long as can be. Count many blessings.

12 / TRUNK

EXIT BOURNE AND THE PEACE MELTS. AS SOON AS YOU start turning, stopping, and going different places again, time becomes king. All the little demands you forgot about start yelling all over. The signs. Go this way. Watch out for these. Definitely watch out for these. Take this. Always too many signs to read safely. I slow down, calculate, and exit off Bourne Bridge. If safety's the issue, there should never be over three signs to read right before a rotary. Circle the WELCOME TO CAPE COD sign and gun the straightaway. Roll windows down and smell ocean air. As strange as it may seem and easy to forget, this is home too. Make the right into Kathy Gates Way and find the lime-green house with gray shutters. Park and hop out to 98A. Double back for the rabbit-foot keys.

Buddy comes down from his attic and opens the screen door. Short white hair, tortoiseshell frames, a houndstooth bathrobe, and track shorts, he looks like he reads the entire newspaper every day.

Nobody followed you? Buddy asks. We shake hands.

No, sir. He jumps in and pulls the emergency brake. Buddy's an artist. Makes woven rugs and baskets. He broke up with his fiancée and there's some stalking concerns, hence me the live-bait decoy driving his car to the Cape.

Great, great, great. He puts a finger to his glasses and looks around. *She's the type to hire a private investigator to find out where I live or something, you know.*

That's wild.

Well within the realm of possibilities, unfortunately. I was low when we met. Suicidal probably. The whole thing was a mistake.

What's in the trunk? I had to ask.

A blanket and a spare. Maybe a flare, but it doesn't open anymore so . . . Why?

Poo-poo face. Henry is buddy's name. Henry wheels me to the ferry, and I miss the last boat by a few minutes. He offers to let me crash at his place, but I pass. Enough adventure for one day, I lie and wait it out in the bus shelter. See some headlights pull up. Henry again.

You sure you okay? He squints. *I feel bad.*

The café opens in a few, I reassure him. *I'm fine.*

Oh. He takes an envelope up off the passenger seat. *Forgot to pay you.*

My God. I hop to. *'Preciate that.* I was so caught up in the ex-fiancée fiasco, I forgot to collect the monies.

Karma good, I camp out for the night and take note of what I can. New City takes such a consistent and abnormal toll on you that you get used to it. The Cape and Islands are so natural and not aggressive that they feel how silence must sound. I read and write myself in and out of naps until first light.

First ferry gears up as me and a couple wait on line. Heavy wind gusts slap us around. Attendant waves us forward, and we walk to the loading ramp with our tickets out. Walking up the plank over molten green seas, I notice a tall father with his daughter on the upper deck. Brave souls. The ocean laps against the ferryboat half playful and half menacing. Try not to look straight into the water's blank expression. She may appear less fierce and evoke a sailboat sense of adventure in the morning, but that's just a baited hook. The horn sounds and the ferry ships off past summer-home coastlines, shrink-wrapped yachts, and bright buoys of red and green. Sun rays poke through a lone hole in the lambswool clouds. A varsity footballer sneaks a cell phone photo. Twenty minutes in with nothing but ocean both ways, the ferry finally arrives at that deep-sea, nothing-but-us-out-here, point-of-no-return feel. It's appropriate, given the last few months of my life. Has it been a year even? Movies make it seem like the point of no return is somewhere near the beginning, but it's not. The point of no return is as far from the beginning as it is the end. That's the point. Even if you wanted to turn back, it would cost you just as much as it would to finish, so you might as well continue. School's out, suckers. For years this boat ride meant summer, a holiday, or a school vacation. In foggy days such as today, this sluggish float across the Vineyard Sound means going home. It's a trip how life's most sacred places can shape-shift right under your nose. Something about the salt air of the Atlantic freshens the spirit. On a day as fog as today, when the rest of known world beyond a few feet is white as a blank page, I feel alive. Seagulls materialize out of oblivion and glide alongside ferry winds.

AWAY

1 / LOVE

THE FOG IS BRIGHT AND OTHERWORLDLY. DON'T SEE
many other travelers besides folks who have to on days as foggy as
today. Time spent traveling reminds me people who want to travel
move in a different dimension than people who need to travel. Fog
this dense becomes bizarre. It turns the whole world into a small
white amphitheater. Everything is suddenly only a few things, and
perfectly illuminated. Fog this thick doesn't allow you to hide at
all. Ferryboat powers around and backs into what we must imagine is Vineyard Haven. We dock and I disembark. Hold my breath
through the thick of diesel smoke and walk a wobbly exit ramp. I
stop in the steamship building to pay my respects to Uncle Bird.
Uncle Bird used to work at the dock loading boats, and a local
painter memorialized him in a mural above the ticket counter
front and center with a broomstick gripped like a golf club.

I see police lights out front and a young man on his phone next
to his vehicle. Obviously agitated, he turns back toward the cop
car, and I see it's a kid I used to work with at the grocery store. The
Oak Bluffs bus pulls up to the circle and I exit the steamship.

Yo, dog. Andy waves me over. *Why people want to power trip?* He seems genuinely concerned.

I shrug.

Do me a favor, dog. He waves me closer. *Give this to my sister, please.* He offers up a cell phone. *Tell her I'll be at the Edgartown jail.*

I look to the officers, but they're no help.

I'm not positive, but I'm pretty sure I got an outstanding warrant. He shrugs.

I check with the cops again, but no help at all, so I pocket the phone and hop to. *I gotta catch this bus.*

Good looking out, fam.

I buy a new bus ticket, sit in front, and watch as kid's cuffed and escorted to the squad car. We circle the circle, cruise through Five Corners, and bus the road to Oak Bluffs. Strong winds lean against us crossing the drawbridge. There's a break in the fog, and a pinhole of strong sun peeks through. Unpocket buddy's phone and call his sister. I let her know he'll be in Edgartown and wish her happy holidays. Open the faulty phone case and peep four hundred-dollar bills and a glassine. *Greeeat.* I stash and look around, but it's just me, the driver, and a lady with a well-decorated walking staff. Pull the yellow cord before gas station and driver drops me off. Walk Munroe and the sandy dirt road home.

The Highlands smell like dirt, salt, and trees. White folks call the Highlands East Chop. We call it the Highlands. The history is different. As odd as it may seem now, more than Hartford or New City, the Highlands is home. Annie, my little cousin, looks out the kitchen window. She's a small person already.

June is heeeya, she says, running to the door. *June, guess what?*

She opens the screen. *We saw a mama deer and a baby deer. And the baby was right outside Nana's window!*

Aren't you lucky? Was it big? I give her a hug and an Uncle Bird kiss. *Where's Puda?*

Nana's sitting in her room in her chair reading the *Hartford Courant.* I drop my bags by the wobbly table in the living room.

Hey, babes. She stands up and gives me a hug and a kiss. *I'm so happy to see you, you don't even know.*

Brook walks in, picks Annie up, goes back to her room, and slams the door. Brook's my aunt. A little less than two years older than me, she was like a sibling growing up.

What's wrong with her? I have to ask.

We had to go to court to try to get Puda back. Nana tears up. *So we're in a little emotional limbo here.*

Court? Where?

And this is home too. And school. It's like life-home-school. Vacation never felt like vacation for me. Every time I went home there was another fire to put out. Something new, something slightly tragic and ridiculous. Rarely for the good. This time is court and kids and safety, or lack thereof. Brook took the kids off-Island to go shopping, and things went left. Nana picks her paper back up.

I don't know, June. Her new medication is throwing her for a loop.

Brook's narcoleptic.

I think that might have more to do with it than we'd like to admit, but that's another story for another time. When they asked her to do the breath test, dingbat told them no.

Oh God, I say.

Oh yeah.

Brook walks back into Nana's room and sits on the edge of the bed. *You told him?* she asks.

Nana turns the page. *I think maybe it'd be best if you told him, seeing how it's your story and all.*

I don't know why. Brook frowns. *You tell him everything anyways.*

Slamming doors as if you own the place, Nana continues.

I can't waaait to move back to Hartford. Brook brings her palms together in prayer. *Lord, please. Please let me get my life together so I can get off this island.*

Nana rolls her eyes. *See what I'm dealing with here?*

Oh yeah, 'cause June is sooo perfect. Brook stands and has a belly laugh.

Oh, the water was choppy and a lot of fog, but other than that my trip was great, thanks, I say.

Nana and Brook fight often. They're both oddly dependent on each other and strong-willed, and now Brook has two young kids who depend on the both of them as well.

Brook crosses her arms. *I think she's trying to drive me crazy.*

Like you were raised in a barn or something, Nana says from behind her paper. *I don't understand how manners is too much to ask for nowadays.*

What do you want me to do, Ma? Gee whiz. I'm going through a lot right now. Do you understand? It's like everything I do is wrong to you. Lord, please let me get my life together.

Hopefully. Nana's now looking at me. *So we been working with the lawyer to get Puda back,* she says. *Again, emotional limbo. Right or wrong, who are you to decide you have the right to take a child from his family? What gives you the audacity to assume such authority? To take a child from his home?*

You might as well tell him about the mortgage too. Brook chomps on a saltine cracker.

Nana folds her paper together. *Will you let me finish speaking for once? I told him weeks ago!*

If I could describe her expressions accurately, I would. Nana speaks with her eyes the way Italians use their hands. She speaks with her hands too, but she's handling the *Courant.*

So nooow, Nana sings, *we need to settle up with the lawyer aaand the mortgage.*

Brook chomps. *And your health insurance is going up next month. That's what they say.*

They can't do that, can they? I ask. My turn to catch the crazy eye.

Five hundred a month, Nana says.

Brook lies back and rests on Nana's bed. *These people are crooks.* She stares at the ceiling and sits back up, suddenly excited. *I just remembered we got them ribs from Friday.* She heads out. *Throw some corn on the grill too, baby. That's what's up, yo.*

Annie's been sitting quietly on the couch, but food talk inspires action. *I wanted checkin, Mom!*

Well, you ate all the damn chicken yesterday, greedy. What you want? Me to make another one like I made you?

Nana laughs and turns the page. *Happy holidays,* she says.

The matriarch of generations holding on to the thinnest of seemingly indestructible threads. Without fathers or father figures, the living is often improvised and dangerously close to disaster, but we make it work somehow. That's home too. An element of the miraculous is always at play. God knows we don't always deserve it. Annie talks Brook into chicken, and we eat a quiet Thanksgiving dinner. Quiet for us. The holidays don't feel right without Puda, but this is home too. We make our peace. Jackson, Nana's new beagle, sits in a corner by the window. I scrape my plate, thank Brook, and give Nana the mortgage money in an envelope.

Thank you, darling. She tucks it away.

I kick off before she need say any more and take a shower. Sit down with Annie at the kitchen table and draw. She colors in crayon until she passes out, cheek to table.

Brook runs out her room with the phone. *Puda coming back Tuesday!* she says.

Hear Nana get up out her chair. They hug and cry. Annie wakes up, no idea what's going on, and hugs legs.

2 / PATIENCE

Wake up early to Jackson licking my face. I hop to, shower, dress, and step out. *I'll be back, Nana.*

Okay, darling. She's already into today's paper.

I walk to town and hit Circuit Avenue. The fog is back. Circuit Avenue is Main Street or Broadway basically, but the Vineyard is so seasonal that during the off-seasons Circuit Avenue's a ghost town.

I field a call from Hollywood. *Yeeer.*

What's good, froggy? he says. *What's the Island look like?*

Dead. You already know. Hollywood went to high school out here.

Already. Hollywood coughs up a lung. *How's Nana?*

She's good. Brook had an accident with Puda in the whip and she wouldn't do the breath tests or something, so the cops called social services and they been dealing with that.

That's all bad.

All of it. It's like seven stories in one, and none of it is good.

Passing car honks and slows to a stop. It's Hollywood's mother, Fergy.

And your mother just rolled up, I tell him.

Tell her to answer her jack, he says.

A "jack" is a phone.

Fergy's got a headful of beautiful dreads, freckles, and all types of accessories.

Your mother told me you was on-Island, Fergy scolds. *I could have picked you up from the boat you know.*

It's all good. Hug and a kiss. *Here.* I hand her my phone. *Somebody want to talk to you.*

Oh God. Fergy takes it up. *Hello. Who is this?* Fergy's car is white with a maroon peace sticker on the hood and varsity-red interior. *Don't try to check me, son! I called and left you a message, so where you been? Chump.*

I fall out laughing.

Listen, I have to go pick up the girls. I don't have time to school you. She hands me back the phone. *You need a ride?*

I'm okay. I thank her.

Fergy waves and wheels off. I walk around East Chop and watch the boats bob. I drift with the ships passing in the distance. See a seal. Phone rings and it's my bro J. Luis. Walk to his house and they're partying like it's the Fourth of July. A welcome break from depression central. We chop it up, grub, and watch nonsense on television.

What's good with the city? J. Luis asks.

J. Luis is an actions-speak-louder-than-words type of guy. He says what he means, and he sees things from a very grounded yet creative perspective.

A whole lot for a little man, I tell him. *You know the city. I'm lowkey thinking about moving back to the Island at this point.*

Honestly—J. Luis shrugs—*the rock ain't bad as long as you got something to occupy your mind. And you wild creative already.* He shrugs again. *What's good with Hollywood?* he asks. *Y'all still at New City Public?*

Yessir. He chillin' and doing daddy duties. Z growing up so fast.

I know she is. My little girl just turned three.

Three!

Crazy, right? J. Luis smirks and drops a pistachio shell in the ashtray. *Time flying like a booger.*

I spit some of my drink out laughing.

Speaking of time. He shows me an email on his phone. *People must want a throwback or something. Remember that reality show they wanted us on?*

Nooooo.

Yup.

A network was looking for a Vineyard crew to follow for the summer and somehow heard about us. We had a few meetings in the city and screen tests, but they ended up going with a young group of Italians from the Jersey Shore. I was upset at the time of course, but thank God now in hindsight.

Crazy, right? We'll see how this one goes. How's Joy doing?

She's great. Working and staying low. You know her.

They went to high school together. We catch up and have a good time laughing with Big Jos and Chris.

J. Luis wheels me back to the house, and Brook's in the kitchen window in a bra with a hair wrap.

Who's that, J. Luis? She waves as he salutes quietly and backs down our sandy dirt road.

3 / WHY

YOU SEEN YOUR MOTHER? **BROOK ASKS ME.**

You mean your sister?

Yeah. Brook greases her own scalp. *She supposed to finish my hair tonight.*

Brook shows me the back of her head, which clearly she cut herself.

Yikes.

Shut up, June. She laughs.

Nana steps out with her walker, and I hit the bathroom to wash my hands.

Felisha here? Brook yells.

Nana's in the fridge. *What?*

Felisha. Is she here? Felisha is one of Ma's good Island friends.

Oh Lord, Nana says.

Why would I know that? I ask.

'Cause we supposed to fight when she get here. Brook checks out the window.

You ready? I tease her.

Yup. She points to the dresser. Sure enough, there's Vaseline, hair scrunchies, and a hammer.

Nana shakes her head. *I'm going back to bed. Good night.*

Night, Nana.

She think I'm playing. Brook checks out the kitchen window.

You sure you don't want to consider another course of action? She already made her peace.

Luckily, Felisha never shows. I get some writing in. It occurs to me revisiting some of these highs and lows that I haven't told anyone close about my current in-between-lease-ness. Feels like the kind of thing you should tell friends or at the very least family. It also feels worlds away. Maybe the truer version is that illuminating my great failure openly is too much for me to deal with right now. It's very possible. All I know ultimately is that I feel such a sense of relief to not have to worry about where I'm resting my head today. Thank you, God. A nap would feel good right now. I haven't *slept* slept in a minute. Finish my journal page, pack up, and crash.

Wake up to the rumblings of a taxi van out front the house.

Who's that out there? Nana's in the kitchen baiting Annie. *Who's that?*

Annie runs to the door. *Aunty Mimi, Aunty Mimi, Aunty Mimi's he-yooor!*

Ma walks in with a pink duffel and matching suitcase. I hop to, hug, and help her with her luggage.

What's up, boy? she says.

Same old. You know me.

Ma looks happy. She brings a whole other energy to the house and bridges so many gaps. It's a lighthearted wisdom and playfulness. I don't know how long it's been since I've seen my mother. A year? Two? As usual after an abnormally long absence, we tell stories, reminisce, and laugh for hours.

4 / MEET

THE CROWS WAKE YOU UP IN THE HIGHLANDS. THEY roll deep; they're shiny, black, and large as cats; and they tear through your trash and knock over recycling bins if you don't pay proper dues. What's proper this week or the next depends on the crow mafia's mood. Individually, crows know how to open just about anything. If, collectively, they really want to get at something, they'll find a way.

Ma steps out the bathroom with Brook's head wrap, a black hoodie, and jeans. *You ready?* she asks.

Let me brush my teeth. I feign readiness. Somehow between awake and asleep, I agreed to go to an AA meeting, and today is the day.

So you just gonna dog me out on my hair? Brook asks.

"Dog me out" = leave me hanging or in limbo.

I'll do it when we get back, Ma promises.

Yeah, okay. Brook's not buying it.

For real. Ma's faux enthusiasm sounds nowhere near convincing.

We walk the Highlands and cross New York Avenue toward the library. We hook that left just before School Street and enter

church building. AA MEETING UPSTAIRS, sign says. We ascend
to the second floor.

When it's Ma's turn to speak, she passes. I can see she's nervous
with the beginnings of sweat on her nose. I can see she wants to
speak. I feel her pain as a son, knowing how hard it must be for her
to want to pass and to speak. I wait, hoping she finds the courage
to say things she needs to say as she asks politely to pass. The AA
folks don't let her off the hook. Technically, they should, but they
don't. AA on a small island is anything but anonymous, and the
rules are a bit different. Reluctant, shaken, and refused, Ma finally
shares her story. She doesn't tell the details, but she gives the views.

And now I'm here, thank God. She laughs. *Two days after
Thanksgiving with ten dollars to my name trying to take it one day at
a time.*

Amen, a small crew says.

Rest of the group is what you'd expect from an island of north-
easterners. Prideful, broken, and here today. There are a few pleas-
ant surprises, but it's mostly self-proclaimed drunks and druggies
who wanted a little more than what they got, and got stuck chasing
a false feeling of happiness. After a while this second-floor church
room begins to reek of rotted dreams. From the candied carpet
to the sinking eyes. Some are young and fresh from last night's
bender. Some seem to have a handle on their sobriety and come
for the metaphysical conversation, company, coffee, and cigarettes.

One guy arrives super late and made-for-TV with muddy boots
and shaky hands. He dives to a seat in the far corner and nearly
breaks the chair. He's small and thin, but there's so much energy
within and around him it almost makes no sense. His eyes are dark

and unapproachable. Something's eating him alive inside like a fire he can't put out.

This guy's a train wreck, I whisper to Ma.

Aaaw. She's sympathetic. *That's my buddy Dave. He's a sweetheart.*

The AA format is mostly open for anyone to share or not share, and when given the opportunity, Dave declines with little opposition. Most of the AA folks are NA as well, and here they pretty much all know each other. Dave can't take the sitting for too long and attacks the coffee station. Everyone kind of waits for him to get his coffee before continuing by talking slower with less intent. Dave can't not slam things. The meeting wraps, and folks step outside for cigarettes. Ma and I cross School Street to the library. It's a little tripped out how early it is still. After something as heavy as an AA meet, you expect the sun to have dropped already. It's not even noon.

After the library we walk to town to pick up some groceries from the Brazilian market and run into Doc and his father having a father-son breakfast at Slice.

Look who the cat dragged in. Doc stands, and we hug. *Sky-walker,* he says.

Doc's called me Skywalker since I was twelve. No clue why.

He wipes his mouth. *Poppa was just telling about his* new *girl-friend.* He laughs loud. *Met this one on the ferry.*

Who Melissa? Poppa asks. He's hard of hearing.

Yes! Doc yells. *Talking about your new girlfriend!*

Poppa sips his tea. *Women.*

Say goodbye, and Ma and I walk back toward the Highlands.

In regular life Doc is president of one of the most prestigious Ivy League programs in the country. On the Vineyard he's free to be his true self, which is hilarious and super Black.

Seem like everybody's on-Island today, Ma says.

I think people are starting to move here for real.

Is that what it is? She doesn't buy it.

Think so.

I wouldn't. Ma laughs. *This island is too smaaall. Too many people in your business.*

It's also very lonely, harsh, cold, and depressing in the winter. The summer population balloons to 150,000 and it feels like a resort, but in the off-seasons and particularly the winter there are fewer than 15,000 people here and you have no choice but to face yourself consistently.

We gotta stop by Bear Paw's grave, Ma says.

Bet.

We hook a left up to Oak Grove past the church and the library again. So much has changed since Bear Paw, my great-grandfather, passed, yet still it feels very much the same. We still don't have a car to get around in, which is comical to me. I close my eyes and connect with him. Everybody's still struggling to be good and do right and keep up. I guess it's the way it should be. I do my best to convince him I'm doing my best. Bear Paw believed in me before I could speak, so I guess I'm more or less trying to convince myself. I been racking up a lot of losses here, I level with him, and the wins are few and far in between. I get as close to my truth as possible and feel relieved knowing Bear Paw's natural reactions. I pray for him and his wife, Bobbi, who's buried next to him. Everyone I can think of I pray for. I confess my homelessness and the reasons for my stubbornness. I promise to fix his garden out front. I open my eyes and see Ma searching her purse. She pulls out her phone.

Hello, darling! She answers like Nana and laughs. *Wait . . .* Ma looks around. *Don't lie to your mother, fool. Don't you know you go to hell for that?*

Joy's jeep wheels down the Oak Grove Cemetery road and pulls up alongside of us.

Hey, hey. Joy smiles.

Hey, baby! Ma laughs.

We hop in. Hugs and kisses. *What's up with y'all?*

Visiting Bear Paw, Ma says.

Sounds wild, but I forget how refreshing it is to see my sister. We know each other best, I'm sure. I have dreams where we speak in a language with no words, and I'm pretty sure she understands me without explanation as well.

What's up with you? I ask Joy.

Same old, she says. *Just riding around getting ready for the madhouse.*

Truuue. Ma laughs. *Mad it is.*

We drive home and spend quality time together. It is mad, but it's also us. What can you do?

Monday, Ma and Joy leave for work and we say our sad goodbyes. Tuesday it's my turn. I try to wait as long as I can to see Puda, but I have to get back to the city.

What time's your boat? Nana asks from behind her newspaper.

Pack my messenger. *Two thirty-five,* I tell her.

Annie runs to the kitchen window. *Your taxi's he-yoor!*

Nana. *She's a sharp one, honey.*

You can't take a later boat? Brook asks.

Gotta catch a boat, bus, and train. Hug, kisses, wallet, phone, and keys.

You make it look good, son, Nana says. *Take your time. It'll aaall work out.*

I will. I love you, Nana. Ciao, bella!

Oh, I love you too. Hugs and kisses. *Ciao, bella! Que belle luna!*

Y'all stupid. Brook laughs. *Have a safe trip.*

I will. Give her a sloppy Uncle Bird kiss.

Ewww!

Call us when you touch down, Nana says.

I will.

Ferryboat is far less romantic coming back. Two hairy and unruly dogs keep trying to force me into friendship. Makes my throat itch. I change seats. Boat feels heavy. Burdened. Lonely, lonely ferry. A little girl enters from outside. Parents give her two quarters to turn a penny in a grinding, cranking, disturbing souvenir machine. Dock in Woods Hole. Disembark. The bus to New City via Boston's parked up. Step on and catch a seat by myself. Definitely the silver lining. Lady asks how long before we leave.

Got 'bout a half hour, driver says.

Remember I still need to print my ticket. Step off and walk to Ahab's Café. My new goal is to be honest about what I'm feeling, and at this point I don't have a clue. Lonely and confused maybe. Fractured. The way I see it, either I have three hometowns or none. Either I'm from a few places or none. What I'm certain of is, I've taken this bus so many times I should own stock, as Grandpa likes to say. I smell my armpits and remember I need to put on deodorant.

5 / BOGEY

WALK TO AHAB'S RESTROOM TO PUT ON DEODORANT, buy bus ticket online, and print for less than a dollar. Fifteen bucks cheaper than the steamship. Start back toward the bus and stop before a wooden Native American sculpture. Whoever carved it was drunk and/or racist. Step inside and notice the price of cigarettes in Massachusetts is half that of New City. Tempted to buy a pack just for the value proposition. Talk myself out of it and double back for a carton or two.

That going to be all for you? clerk asks.

Can't tell if she's joking as I nervously stuff three cartons into my duffel and walk toward the bus. Reclaim my seat and melt away. Trees and trees. Darkness. Cape Cod. Boston. After a while it's just trees, time, and space. Step off in Boston and wash my hands. Lean up against a wall in South Station and charge my cell. There's a drunk behind me tripping out, and I pay him no mind until I realize it's buddy from AA. Ma's guy Train Wreck Dave. Reboard my bus before he recognizes me and carry on. Seat by myself again. Darkness. Reading light. Trees, night sky, oceans of open road, red and white lights, and yellow guidelines.

Bus stops in North Haven, 6:42 p.m. on the bulb matrix. Wait in Darby's line behind dude with a shiner and buddy all stitched up. There was a fight at a concert they can't stop talking about. Buy a turkey ranch sandwich and a large coffee, $5.79, and eat on the bus.

6 / STATES

SAME BUS STOP IN NORTH HAVEN WHEN I SEE A PAIR of headlights creep around the parking lot toward us like a shark with glowing eyes. I can't describe it properly, but I feel a panic build that I've never felt before. Suddenly, midbite in these strange headlights, I feel exposed and vulnerable. I feel like a fraud. That's it. I feel like the ultimate fraud about to get exposed. I look around, hoping no one sees me. I can't see much and it feels like I'm naked. *Look at that,* my soul seems to say. *Look at that.* Driver exits Darby's and walks toward us. Headlights wheel past him.

If you feel a strange conversation happening inside of you, I journal, *is it you or . . . ?* The more I write, the more I realize the feeling of fraudulence isn't me so much as it is New City reaching out to me. The contrast that is and the grandeur of New City it seem to be reaching out across state lines to remind me of how far I've got to go. From two states away my New City anxieties are reclaiming me. Driver finishes his bogey and keys himself in. He counts the handful of passengers, and we wheel back onto the interstate.

Is someone sitting here? a bundled-up young woman asks me.

Look around to see if I'm tripping.

Not at all.

The bus is relatively empty. I don't look directly at her, but she smells good. She takes off her coat and checks her phone, and I steal a few glances. No idea what she's doing on public transportation, let alone sitting next to me, but thank you, God.

I thought you would come talk to me. She sighs. *You didn't, so I had to come to you.*

A million thoughts and none all at the same time. Adrenaline is the best of it.

That's funny, I say. *I never really pay attention when I travel. Where you coming from?*

New York. She removes her skully. *Headed back now.*

Our knees knock and you would think she wrote me a four-page love letter the way I feel. My goodness.

Asya's her name. A stage name I'm sure. Her mother lives on the Cape, grandma's sick, and it's a last-minute holiday trip. We talk for over an hour. I don't know what drug us together on this bus or why, but here we are.

Asya props her knees up on the seat before us, leans back, and sighs, bored. She fishes a pack of gum out her handbag.

You want? she offers.

No thank you. Am I boring you? I ask her. Asya laughs no, pulls her shoulders back, and cracks her neck.

Looked like it.

Is that what this looks like? She turns off my reading light.

We do all types of wildness somewhere in my mind. Perhaps in hers as well. Every young man on a bus dreams of one day running into an empty one with a beautiful and mysterious stranger, and I've taken this bus hundreds of times. I don't know why but whenever I'm on the verge of an anxiety attack my long-lost dreams come true. A kaleidoscope of graffiti cliffs usher Asya and me into Stamford and New City. Bus pulls into the station. *Okay then*, she says. *That was interesting. Thank you.*

No, no. Thank you. I kiss her on the cheek. *Nice meeting you, Asya.*

Perfect timing, I get a text from Hollywood and the boys to meet up at Asian Public. We disembark, hug, and part ways. I double back to get her phone number and walk to train to Astro Place feeling like the richest man in the world. Then I smell one of the worst smells I've ever smelled. Classic New City–style underground ambush. I can't tell which scribe it is, but the odor is so pungent I have to switch cars. I don't know if it's the lingering smell or just life back in New City, but I can't breathe too well. Aboveground on Third Avenue begin to feel much better in the fresh air, if you want to call it that. I can smell Asya again. Get to Public and the gang's all here. Drop my bags and run up on Row taking pictures of an early man down. *Send me that, please.* Eat someone's fries.

June! She wops.

Walk to bar for a ginger. I'm standing there waiting with everyone having a good time when suddenly I start to feel super low. It's so bizarre and sudden, I wonder if I'm having a medical issue. Or is this just being an introvert? Alone in a crowded room. Either way, the fear of what lies ahead takes the air out of the room. On cue, a mob of New City University first-years file in through the front door and by sheer numbers and mobbish oblivion push me farther down the bar queue. The naive glee does not help.

7 / REGRET

Hollywood enters to a standing ovation and walks over to me at the end of the bar, where I'm hanging on for dear life.

What's good, froggy?

Waiting on a ginger. I force a smile. *And having a mini meltdown in the process. What's good with you?*

Hollywood waves the bartender to. *You been waiting awhile?* He's genuinely confused.

Fellas. A.K. puts arms around us.

Yo, miss! Hollywood yells. *Two gingers, please! Thank you. Thank you. Two gingers! You heard me? Yeah. Thank you. Thank— You want something, Kane?* he asks A.K.

Bartender serves up and I take a sip.

This's Sprite. Table it.

Yo! A.K. *Y'all see that Spanish joint by the hostess?*

Come on, A., Hollywood says. *I knew you locked in on that as soon as we walked in.*

She's probably the baddest I've seen in here.

Who's that?

They point me to her.

Hard to argue.

Hollywood. *It's more the way she carry herself. She got that wave. That butterfly effect.*

A.K. *That's a fact. Magic dust.*

What's good, bro? Hollywood asks me. *You gucci?*

Word. Last time I seen you this serious—A.K.'s eyes light up— *you was listening to Coltrane gazing out the dorm room windows eating a blueberry muffin.*

We were roommates in boarding school while I was working on my first novel and all I ever listened to was jazz. I loved the view from that window. It was a bay window or whatever you call the ones you sit in and look down on the world.

I took the bus back from Martha's Vineyard this afternoon, I confess. *Just got back like an hour ago.*

Road lag. Hollywood shakes his head.

Gingers come again. Sip. *Miss!* Catch her before she flees. *This has something in it. I just want a ginger ale, please.* Bartender apologizes, dumps, and pours up a new one.

On the house. She waves my money away.

Thank you. Leave her a dollar. *So the bus is pretty much empty,* I continue my confession. *Me, the bus driver, and a few people. A woman comes and tries to sit next to me.*

That's the worst!

Usually. I start to feel better just telling the story. *I look up and she got the white-sweater joint from the movies. Super bad. I mean*—take another sip—*you don't see woman this bad in real life.*

Make shorty up front look like a Barbara Bush. Perfect everything. You know how she says hello? "Why didn't you speak to me?" And she got a little attitude.

Yoooo. A.K.

Hollywood. *Come on, man.*

If I'm lying I'm flying. A dancer from Scorers. Seem like every five minutes she's peeling off another layer, stretching and sighing like she's bored to death. Son, super-flat stomach, flawless hip-to-waist ratio, work-of-art figure. Maaaan.

My son, you gotta be the luckiest bum in America.

We fall out laughing.

After a while we playing footsies and kneesies. Finish my ginger ale and ask for another.

So what happened?

That's what happened, I say.

You booked it? Why you ain't try to book her? Hollywood smirks. *He lying.*

She told me her grandmother just died. I think she was on shrooms or something. It just didn't feel right.

A.K. *Honestly, you disappointing me right now. The way you told that story I expected a lot more out of it, my G.*

You got the number at least? Hollywood.

I did get the number.

My phone buzzes as if it knows we're talking about it. Unpocket expecting Asya and see a photo of Puda with a black eye cheesing extra hard. *Puda's back!* Brook text. Smile and show the fellas.

Puda! Hollywood buys a round to unify the night. *We still highly disappointed in you, B. You supposed to book that.*

Phone rings again and it's an unknown number from California.

Hello?

Juney?

Hey. Who's this?

This is Meka!

Who? I walk outside so I can hear.

Meka. Your sister.

Meka? Meka. My older sister on my father's side whom I haven't seen since I was five or six. I'm lying. I flew out to California to visit Pop when I was twelve or so. Pop was monstrosity bent and locked up before my flight back to Connecticut. It was one of those trips that's hard to believe and easy to forget. Hell, that was twenty years ago.

Crazy, right?

Meka laughs and I remember. I remember her laugh. I remember my father's laugh. I remember.

If you down for it, Juney, I can go ahead and connect y'all.

I don't know what I'd . . . I hesitate. *What am I supposed to say to that? I guess I will. Why not? Of course.*

Dude . . . She tells me some of what they've been through and how it was out west. She tells me how Pop has changed. *He's been sober nine years!* She sounds proud.

That's great news. I'm happy for her. *So how you been, Meka?*

I got five beautiful kids.

Five?

Five! And you know what, June? Pop is the best granddad you could ever ask for.

I don't doubt it. How's Bam-Bam?

Bam-Bam! She laughs. *I haven't heard that nickname in years.*

It's what we used to call my younger brother Jay, 'cause even when he was in diapers he was strong enough to move coffee tables with one hand.

Bam-Bam is starting linebacker for Cal State, Meka says.

What?

Yup. Defensive captain. Talk about valleys and peaks.

You know what, Meka—if you set it up, I'm happy to catch up with Pop. Why not, right?

Oh, this makes me so happy, June! I'mma call Pop right now and hit you back.

Right now?

Oh, it's late out there, huh? Let's do it tomorrow, then.

Tomorrow is better.

Okay, bro. I'll talk to you then. Love you, June!

Love you too, Meka. Give the tribe a hug and a kiss for me.

It's a powerful mix of past and future. Excitement feels to be the best of it. Possibility maybe. It's a lot. I don't feel like the same person after we hang up. I feel like I'm approaching a valley I've stood before many times. It's a large valley. It overpowers any idea of getting past it. After our phone call I feel the same valley that held so much nothing now with the potential to yield. I feel like I'm standing before that godforsaken void and watching it fill with rain until there's no longer a valley at all but a surface, a passing that can be crossed by a worthwhile vessel. I never really judged Pop in an adult way. His absence hurt, but I could never sit with it long enough to blame him. How do you sustain blame for someone who isn't there? It was unfortunate, of course, but certainly not unique. I know how, I guess. What I'm really asking is, Why? To what end? I was always taught to do the best I can with what

I have in front of me, and that blame is as powerful a drug as any. I remember crying when I was younger because I held on to the hope that life would right itself somehow, and it did not. I cried and then I learned to deal. It's no surprise I gravitated toward the power of cool and negative space in my creativity. I composed sketches and wrote stories detailing everything but the point. This must be my inner child, I'm now realizing, crying to be picked up.

I'm sitting under New City scaffolding thinking all this and grateful for the most part when something knocks the wind out of me. It's like in the very moment I'm crossing from one major event into another I can also feel everything I've ever stood for become debatable and the ground begin shaking beneath me. Hoping my art hasn't suddenly become spiteful and mundane, I'm mostly reassured in revisiting most of it that I've been fortunate enough not to have based my expressions in what I did or did not possess. In some ways the negative space was also my means of preserving hope. By not defining the void, perhaps I was allowing room for nature to speak for itself.

A sloppy freshman stumbles up to me and slobbers on my blazer.

You got a loosie? he asks.

Someone should have cut you off. Reach for my pack. *How old are you?*

Old enough to drink.

Trade two loosies for a buck. I sit outside for a bit and gather myself before I head back in. Grab my bag and kick off. Cruise the city and take it all in anew. I don't know if it's God, the universe, or just life, but it's certainly funny. It's like I have a new set of eyes and everything looks intentional.

8 / CHANGE

Hit the top floor of New City University library and find a good seat. Hope I run into my young writer friend. Don't. Phone buzzes with a California number.

Hello.

One Love, the voice says.

Pop. I already know. As odd as it sounds, I know his voice exactly.

Man, it's so good to hear you right now. I can't believe Meka found you. She like a bloodhound. How tripped out is this?

It's great to hear from you, Pop. I pack up and sneak out the library. *How did Meka find me?* All my resistance and hesitation melt away at light speed. Whatever iota of me I meant to keep frozen by pride came face-to-face with a star brighter than a thousand suns. Genes are real.

Google, Pop says. *She googled your name and "Brooklyn," I think.*

That's real. I elevator down and step outside to talk. The sun shines bright on me.

I know words can't do nothing more than a dollar can, but let me just tell you how sorry I am.

Walk under oak tree shade.

I'm sorry for not being there for you. I'm sorry I couldn't watch you grow. I'm sorry I wasn't there to help you and your mom. I'm sorry I wasn't there to be your father. You have every right to not accept my apology, and I can't blame you. I just have to say it so you know.

Honestly I kinda wish I wasn't so receptive, but the truth of the matter is that I feel zero animosity or blame toward him. His laugh makes me laugh, and we have the same kind of laugh, which makes us laugh even more. Pop and I catch up as best we can from opposite coasts. There's so much to say and so much to remember. Feels like I've been lost in the grocery store for two decades and someone finally found me. I've had father figures, of course, but there's no replacing your father, and here I now have mine.

Hold up, Juney. Hold up one second. Pop has a quick barter with a scribe and agrees to give him a few bucks if he spends it on food. *Okay. This clown gonna try to play me for Boo Boo the Fool. I'm young, but I wasn't born yesterday. Where were we?*

I don't even know, Pop. We was laughing about Love Lane.

Good old Love Lane. When's the last time you been back?

Years. I drove through with Grandpa not too long ago, but we didn't stop.

What's there to stop for? Unless you trying to get shot.

True indeed. Good old Love Lane.

Man I remember when you used to cross the street. Remember that?

Make sure you look both ways! I do my best Nana and Grandma Billings impersonation. I remember it all. The innocence of it. I remember being Juney. I remember Pop's strength. I remember Grandma Billings's food and her love. The cigarettes and peppermint gum. Both sides of Love Lane.

So when you coming out west, son? Say the word and I got you on the first thing smoking.

Shiiiiii . . . I pretend I'm more game than I am.

There's a mix of fear of disappointment, haste, and drunkenness to deal with. Pop seems to know and understand but still be pushy about it. Feels right. We agree to catch up again soon.

Okay, One. I just want to thank you again, man, and tell you I love you and I'm so glad Meka reconnected us.

Me too, Pop. Love you too.

Aight, One.

One.

I hang up and try to land some of it. Who do I tell? How to explain? Do I even know what just happened? All of what just changed. Float the night full of new winds. Try to keep it simple. *Change,* Nana once said, *is the closest you get to being alive.* Train to Murkt Street before sunrise. Uptown to the school to get a jump on the day. Hit convenience store for a paper, 7:23 a.m., and walk back. Run into Don on his bike as he pedals across Lexington. Walk toward a school bus parked awkward near Mercy Theater. Smoke as thick as fog leaking out from underneath the bus. I look up and see the driver is oblivious.

9 / TAXI

Mr. Deal's chaperoning some rich kids to Greece, so I'm covering his history classes today. That and two periods of gym. They sure do know how to squeeze substitutes good. Elevator up and get started on today's paper. Nothing really worth repeating. Turn pages for my horoscope and see a little mouse run across the floor. Zero students notice. Willful ignorance, I hope. Mouse runs by again. Nobody. First period's easy. Annoying and chatty, but I'll take that over disrespect any day. Second period O.J., my favorite safety agent, comes up with the rubber gloves and 449 and cleans the table off with bleach wipes. She saved me. I was one gag away from chucking.

Thank you.

You know I already know.

What you cleaning for? Chuck asks.

Mind your business, please. Thank you. I try not to laugh.

They supposed to come and lay traps, O.J. whispers to me. *But they say that every year.*

She dips and I scribe in my notebook.

To remember: I'm on my way back from the store and there's a smoking bus pulled over near the theater. The driver's reluctant to let the students off, some kind of liability issue I'm sure, but some good Samaritans convince him otherwise.

Can I go to the bathroom? a young lady asks.
Go 'head.
Can I go? her friend asks.
One at a time.

Students step off the bus as blue flame licks bottom. Students are oblivious but can tell from other faces they need to hustle.

I bag my notebook. *Pop!* Sparks fly from underneath Deal's computer desk. Watch the screen die slow. Class erupts. *What was that? Should we evacuate?*

I'm out of here.

Relaaax. I laugh. *It's a short. Do your work.* To myself, *I swear fire's following me.* The class settles into a laborious quiet.

A student breaks the silence. *I love penguins.*

Penguins are creepy.

Another student throws a pen cap across the room. Aiming for the trash, I assume.

Sorry about that.

Are you really? Y'all buggin' out today. I feign frustration. They really aren't bad at all. I like this class. Goes by fast. Stand out front and say goodbye to the last students leaving.

Vio, our male school safety agent, steps out with me.

Coach. He puts his hands on his waist and stands like a little superhero. *Why you always heeya?* he asks.

It says something when school safety's tired of seeing you.

Go home, he begs.

I'm trying to, I assure him. *Waiting on a friend.*

A female? His beady eyes light up. *And you bring her heeya?* He's suddenly disappointed. *This es no ideal first impression.*

Vio's from Dominica Republic. There and the Lower East Side. His accent is a hilarious mix of Spanish heritage, the city, and willful ignorance.

Is you giiirlfriend?

Jo no say, I kid.

A fire truck screams past and I plug my ears. Two students seated at the curb kiss and hug each other.

O.J. steps out and rolls her eyes. *Meanwhile this one was at the chop shop last week.* Abortion clinic. *Let me go do my sweep.*

O.J. sheaths her radio. *Since I'm the only one concerned about chesters in the building.*

What she mean "chop shop"? Vio asks.

The removal of child.

Still standing like a superhero, Vio makes a sour face.

Teachers kill me. Curbside young girl vents. *It's like if you were anywhere near as intelligent as you put on*—there's a tattoo of an angel falling down the right side of her neck—*you'd actually be teaching us something that mattered. Go help a third world country or something. Seriously. All this common core crap is archaic.*

Occurs to me that she's from somewhere more sunny and wealthy than New City.

If I was a teacher I'd teach students how to get ahead without getting caught, communicate, pretend you care, say "hi," "bye," "thank you," read a lot because that's what really makes you smart, follow your heart, pay attention, live your life, and figure the rest the hell out.

Boyfriend grunts in agreement as they stand and walk. He stuffs an orange book into her backpack and zips it shut.

And make a boatload of money.

Oh, tons.

For such a young face he has an old, dire tone. He may not be from the city either.

Vio smiles at me. *They know ebryting.* He laughs. *But ebryday they heeya.*

A yellow cab jumps the curb and crashes into the handicap railing an arm's length from where the young lovers were sitting. Vio inspects the damage. Young lovers kick off, and I realize she's the same girl who caught the wobbly red kickball that day in the park. The dancer from section B. New neck tattoo. Boyfriend with the boat shoes. Wobbly red kickball. Vio questions the cabbie and jots notes in his book until the Thirteenth Precinct shows up.

Leslie walks up. *Is everything all right?* She gives the scene a look-over.

I hope so.

We hug.

Leslie taught me at Brooklyn College and has remained a friend and mentor. Cops arrive and we observe them, Vio, and the cabbie do the liability dance.

This is a short story at least. Leslie sprinkles magic dust on the happenings.

Cabbie's a twice-married doctor from Albania with a bit of whiplash. Railing needs replacing.

Don walks his bike out, fastening his chin strap. *Dean of students next year. You in, right?*

Absolutely, I confirm.

Leslie nods.

A lot has to happen, obviously. Don looks on at the liability dance. *I'm pretty sure Green's leaving, and I think you'd be great. I'll let you know when we post the position.* Hops on his bike. *In the meantime we need someone to run the back elevator for fifteen to twenty minutes during middle school lunch? Pays a half hour per session?*

Middle school should be time and a half.

Leslie and Don laugh.

I know. Think about it and let me know. See you tomorrow. Don rides off.

Congratulations, I guess. Leslie shrugs. *This is such a great neighborhood.* She smells the air. *Great mix of people.*

It really is, I agree.

O.J. gives me the okay and we bag up. *Let's get out of here before we become witnesses.* Kick off. Chuck, Reem, and crew step out the dollar pizza shop.

Yo, Coach, you subbing tomorrow? Chuck.

Hopefully.

Sub for White, pleeease, Reem pleads. *He's out of his mind.*

They laugh, hit the corner, and see the accident. *What the—*

Language!

10 / ELEVATE

AFTER I KICK OFF FROM LINKING WITH LESLIE, I FEEL recharged. Something about hanging with a writer who actually made it in the city that says *No chance* is super powerful. Makes you feel slightly less crazy. I purchase some contraband snacks, brave the wind, and treat myself to an independent movie across from West Fourth. Lots of life change, huh? ~~Father~~ vs. Father. Home vs. ~~home~~. It's a trade-winds type of winter. The movie is great, and when I exit the theater it's damn near warm outside, with a gentle breeze welcoming me back. As soon as you decide to get over her, New City decides to love you again. I drift for the rest of the night and watch the sun rise comfortably. Walk to Public and run into Don on the way in.

I'll do the back elevator, I tell him.

Excellent, he says. *Wanna start today?*

High school gym day. Nothing out of the ordinary.

Sure.

I commit and within fifteen minutes I learn a valuable lesson about news in schools. By second period, most students and teachers know I'm running the back elevator for middle school lunch.

Aside from the copy-and-paste confirmation conversation I have to have a thousand times, there's also the tickled anticipation-of-tragedy vibe that few can disguise. Stop by Don's office to get the official middle school lunch elevator rundown, raise my hand to knock on the royal-blue door, and hear him and Lacey arguing about next year's dean position. Hold off and listen to my future unfolding. Don's campaigning for me. Lacey's interested in someone from the after-school department. Listen in until it feels kind of wrong, then knock.

Sorry to interrupt. Is there a list of rules anywhere for the back elevator?

They look at each other, confused and amused. Don tells me to check in with the current dean two doors down.

Cool. Thanks.

I walk and see it's the teacher from the french fry incident. I enter the computer lab and ask, but he doesn't have much guidance either. He says they've changed the rules so much that no one can be sure of what exactly to enforce anymore.

I ride the back elevator up and down from the street exit on the first floor to the back of the kitchen on the ninth to get a sense of what's what. The quiet before the storm. Descending to the first, I begin to hear it. The raw sound of adolescent repression and juvenile freedoms colliding with middle school combustions. It's Dante's *Inferno*. The elevator door's still sliding open when they attack.

No way! I yell to those trying to squeeze. *That's enough!*

They continue. In no time I'm helplessly wedged in a corner with my notebook as my only weapon. Math teacher who looks like Jesus happens by, doubles back, and saves my life. He doesn't yell and he doesn't appear to be too upset, but there's a calm fire in his eyes as he explains, after getting everyone off the elevator, the importance of self-awareness and safety in society—especially in close quarters such as elevators. His speech is so inspiring a couple of students volunteer to walk the nine flights up. Seeing them do it, about half of the remaining students follow suit. The door slides to shut, and I thank him from a spacious and peaceful elevator. Drop students on ninth. Elevator stops at random floors, and traffic is far easier to manage. Descend to the first again and hear the wild chants of sugar, social media, faux freedom, and the glee of senselessness. Doors slide open and I stand in front this time. Use my physicality. As a substitute teacher, you're so cautious not to touch anyone you forget your hands also protect you. I give my best math-teacher-esque speech, with credit of course. Mr. Chris is his name, the students tell me. Moment of truth, most students walk on in a semi-orderly pattern until the back of the line falls forward like dominoes. Loud screams and chaos. I make sure no one's hurt and start us over.

Stairs! I yell. *Take the stairs.*

I have an elevator pass.

If you do not have an elevator pass, take the stairs. I write gibberish in my notebook. *Elevator's a privilege you have not earned. Goodbye.* Brushed stainless steel door slides shut.

A few students try to sneak in on other floors, and I shut it down. I feel semi-accomplished until I realize I just turned into the french fry teacher. I descend, 11:49 a.m., one last time into an institutional calm. Door slides open and a pair of suits step on alongside O.J. I don't say anything. O.J. fobs a floor for them and dips. Elevator back down, and that's it. Last of the lasts have been elevated. Motivate to step out for a slice and see O.J. at the front desk.

You working with the feds now? I tease.

I wish. They got them benefits. Those were detectives. She writes in her book. *Don't be surprised if you see Public in the news tomorrow morning.*

Oh no.

Yup. That's why I just mind my business.

Listen. I can't not vent. *That back elevator is naaasty business. Horrible.*

It's Friday too? O.J. frowns with empathy.

I step out for my slice and see a missed call. Voicemail from Nana that Ma's relapsed. I call Joy.

Hey, hey, Joy answers.

Here we go again, I say.

I can't. Dead serious. *I'm on my way there now,* she says. *Crossing the bridge.*

Cool, cool, I say. *Wait. Why?* I ask.

I been traveling for work so much, she says. *Just to be there, I guess. I don't know. I just feel like I should be there.* Check my watch and tell her I'll see if I can make it up as well. Sub last gym class. Realize I can't sub and do middle school elevator every day. It's just too much psychological warfare. Happy to have work but not enough to forfeit my sanity.

Bell rings and people flow out into the city. See Hollywood in a full pink-grapefruit outfit.

What time's the last boat from Woods Hole? I ask him.

To the rock? Nine forty-five.

I might have to make that run, I tell him. *Ma relapsed again.*
That's the worst.

The worst.

Alcoholism is crazy because the only person who actually has any power or agency is the one whose whole being is being possessed. You can try to help. You can talk it out or force the issue. Once that's done and they still can't shake free, all you can really do is let them be and be there for whenever they do find a way to break free.

I scramble after let-out and take the bus up to the Vineyard. Make the last boat, and Joy picks me up from the steamship authority.

Thank you, my dear. I hop in. Hugs and kisses. *How you?*

I don't want to go to work. Joy laughs.

Call out.

Played that game yesterday.

We have different fathers and different last names, but we're twins spiritually. Nana and Ma did most of the raising.

Was the boat choppy?

Not really.

Good.

Joy has Ma's eyes. Her father taught me how to ride a bike and swim, I think. I'm not sure. I remember somebody light-skinned throwing me off a boat.

Aren't you glad to be home? She smiles.

So happy.

We delve into the familial sarcasm. I am kinda happy, though. She is too. We've shared this relapse conversation before.

Joy ended up going to school on the Island and living with

Nana while I was away at boarding school. She came into her own here, yet we're still pretty much the same person. Same motivations. Same humor. Same sense of things.

How many times do you need to . . . you know . . . to finally get it? Joy's genuinely confused. *I feel bad because when Nana told me, it felt like she was defending Ma and that kinda made me angry.*

Same!

Thank God she felt it too.

Same exact thing. I felt horrible. At the same time, Nana has to know she doesn't really have a choice.

That's real. Joy wheels through Five Corners. Fights the sea breeze before the bridge. *It's so heartbreaking.*

Annie's in the kitchen window when we pull up. Joy parks.

Meanwhile, meet Annie, the smartest kid in the world.

Convince Joy to call out of work and take Annie and Puda to the tennis courts off Munroe.

Who knows the score? What's the score? Puda asks.

We're wenning. Annie swings at a bug.

Nobody's keeping score. Joy returns a volley.

Annie laughs hard. *I fink I pooled a hamstwing.*

You can't even spell hamstring.

Yes I can.

Prove—

All right, you two. Joy's not having it. *Everything doesn't have to be a competition.*

Yeah. I back her up. *Little nerds.*

In the morning I walk to the library. Visit Bear Paw's grave and chill at Uncle Bird's bench in Waban Park. Hit the crib. Sometimes talking to Nana, I remember how rare it is to have someone to talk and listen to for all of your life. She's my consigliere. Sometimes we talk and I feel it might be the last time, so I listen to every word. Other times we just chill and watch television. Today is a combo. We talk for hours about dreams and patience, watch TV, and laugh on old stories. What do I take from it? Sometimes, it's clear, listening to Nana and Joy—sometimes you just have to be there. That's all. Your presence. There's nothing any of us could have done, really, other than being there for each other. All the doing and trying is cool, but ultimately it's not up to you. All you can do is show up.

Catch the bus Sunday, and it occurs to me on the way back through blue sky and trees that we hardly spoke about Ma's relapse at all. Sleep through the roadwork. Transfer in Bourne and Providence.

Punch-drunk but well rested, I slowly make my way back to New City Public. Catch an extra impromptu nap in the gym.

I rise and see Peanut working the equipment room door with a red credit card.

You got credit? I walk over to him.

Nah. Peanut laughs. *My father gave it to me.*

Key the door for him. *Basketball?*

Yessir. Thanks, Coach.

Exchange a rock for his credit card.

You got one shot, I prompt. *Midrange. If you miss, you done.*

Confident little ball player, he shrugs and takes a couple dribbles to the corner. Cash.

Meanwhile, let me remind you that there's a kid in the projects in Albania. He don't have no friends, no family, no gym. Just a makeshift pill and a milk crate. And he wants your spot.

Here you go! Peanut laughs. *It's too early for all this, Coach!*
Is it?

I pick up in my notebook and let him shoot. Write it out. If today's back elevator action is too much, I'll tell Don I'm not doing it. Come to some resolve and prep for morning basketball. Two middle school gym classes and I'm back in the swing of things.

Lunch comes and the elevator's not half bad. Nothing like Friday. If I'm being totally honest with myself, it's probably still too much to bear every day. Notebook be my shield and protect me from those who wish to harm me, please. Deflect all sneezes and coughs.

Last trip, 11:51 a.m., not bad at all. I did it. Or so I think. Elevator makes a surprise stop on the second floor. A middle school teacher steps on and passive-aggressively confronts me about my ability to supervise both the elevator and the steps. I tell her she raises some great points, which she should definitely discuss with whoever gets paid to figure these things out.

Walk with Hollywood after let-out to Madison Square and drift out of normal range, which at this point is damn near impossible. Find myself in Center Park looking at folk rowing ratty boats in an artificial pond. Plot on food and realize I have $8 to my name. Life gets real real quick and often these days. I slow down and try to enjoy the last of this great sun. Hell, I remember when $8 was a fortune.

I want a milkshake. An artificial lover materializes. *Or a smoothie.*

Definitely not a milkshake. Artificial lover number two does a good job of bobbing and weaving. *Milkshakes make you thirsty.*

Oh my God, you're so right. Let's get smoothies. Her desire is so pure and selfish I can't get it, yet I understand completely. We walk the same path and pass a sage playing 'Trane's "Alabama" on his saxophone. I pause and listen. The artificial lovers hit the smoothie truck.

Can I have a strawberry, please? lover number one orders.

Medium or large?

Small, please.

Medium and large is all we got.

Large. Thank you. We can share. Are you hungry? Wait, are the bananas ripe or are they green like that? She points to the fruit display.

They're ripe. Will that be all?

That's it. Thank you so much.

Blenders, bangs, and clangs. Smoothie. *Seven forty-nine, please.*

Oh. Do you have cash? lover number one asks. *I didn't bring my wallet.*

I do. He fishes bills out his pocket. Artificial lovers walk back toward the park and again we're on the same path.

What's the matter?

Nothing, lover number two says.

You're in a mood. You've been quiet all day.

That's interesting. I feel fine.

Taste this, she says. *These bananas are the opposite of ripe.* They stop walking.

Got a little bite to it. Not bad. You want to go back?

That's so aggravating. I asked multiple times.

Artificial lover's entire life force is suddenly weighed down by disappointment. The smoothie straw pulls from her lips in slow motion with a string of spit as she lowers the smoothie itself and lobs it to the trash. I'm watching this $7.49 fruit juice rotate like a goddamn buzzer beater. It back-rims into the rusty green rubbish bin, busts open, and bleeds out. Hear the saxophone playing in the distance. It's chilly out. A black squirrel's migrated from Stytown. Artificial lovers carry on, but I'm stuck with it. Everyone's up when you're down in New City. Need to get somewhere in a hurry? New City'll move like molasses. Having a good time? New City will fly by in a minute. I sit on a bench under a lamp next to the wasted smoothie and let the tears flow. I walk. I walk a long ways. End up downtown lost on cobblestones by the African slave memorial. Train back to Gold Street.

What's good, my G? Blue unlocks the gate.

Not much. I need a spot to crash tonight, if that's cool.

Cat runs by chasing something.

I feel some type of way you even asking.

We hit the living room.

Look like you ain't sleep in a month. Big on the rock, so you can crash on your old bed.

Jackpot.

I take it as a spiritual sign and fill up with gratitude. Watch all of five minutes of sports highlights and head to my old mattress. Things got shaky today, but it worked out. I'm sleeping in my own bed.

The morning is a different story completely. Rather than rested and relieved, I feel nervous. Pull the blanket back and feel super itchy. Sit up and realize my breath is super short. I hope I'm tripping or something until I pull back the black sheet separating rooms and see the blanket is caked in cat hair. I'm allergic to cat hair. Bad. I was so tired last night I didn't even check. Judging by the state I'm in by the time I hit the bathroom, today's going to be a long day. What does it feel like? Imagine you're free diving and drift past the point you have oxygen for and the current requires you to fight just to stop, let alone begin your ascent. Wash my hands and face, dress quick, and bounce before I pass out. Chilly morning air helps a bit, but not much.

11 / DANDER

I SURVIVE. AS A KID I USED TO HAVE TO GO TO THE hospital and get steroids to stop the asthma attacks. I almost died twice. The fresh air really works wonders, though. I walk to a New City film academy café and sit up front by the window. People. Rain. Breathe back to not-so-good again. Asthma relapse. Asthma is an odd ailment. Odd and perhaps slippery because you can easily forget about it, as I have, and even think you've outgrown it. Pack up and step out for some fresh air relief again but feel quite the opposite. The density and the New City night urgency and the overarching buildings and the lack of trees all seem to smother me. Step back inside café half suffocating and confused. I'd slept at Gold Street a bunch of times before. Never quite in a cat-hair quilt, but still. The couch can't be that different. Cats love couches. Hell, I figured sleeping in my own bed was a triple win. Panicked and somewhat resigned, I train it to Brooklyn University. Maybe some words will do the trick. The loose plan for someone who never really makes plans makes sense until halfway there I feel like I might actually die before I get there. Only time I can breathe a decent breath's when the doors open. Beat an older woman to a door seat, apologize, and try to keep cool. Disgusted expressions of God knows what I have zero energy to figure out or fight. Actually took most of what I had in me to beat her to the seat. Like I said—extenuating circumstances. Each stop's a battle for one cool, clean breath that stretches the imagination in all the ways it is not. Need some cool fresh air? New City will give you train delays. Four local stops away, I come to terms with the fact that I may have to find a hospital. Meanwhile, people are still pissed I took the old lady's seat. The worst part is I understand. Guy next to me stands and offers her his seat, but she passes and I enjoy the space to breathe a bit better. It's short-lived, as a woman who was playing the door comes and squeezes the life out of me. It gets so bad I try to astral project aboveground and locate a hospital nearby. Doors finally close and my messenger bag feels like a boulder on my lap. I rest it on the floor between my legs and try not to die. Last stop is the slowest arrival. I do my best to stand and wait for the doors to open, but inside I'm in a panic. In my mind, as soon as these doors open I'm stepping off, running up the steps, catching that fresh air, and heading straight to the hospital. The doors finally open and I can barely walk fast enough to not get yelled at. When I reach the steps I'm the sole rider in the station. Weak beyond any previous notions, I crawl up the stairs on my hands and knees.

12 / GRAVE

IT'S AN EMBARRASSING AND DESPERATE ASCENSION, but we make it to the top step and a stream of cooler air. Drop my bag, unbutton my shirt, and try to regroup. Woozy. Rest for a few minutes. Try to stand up and succeed. Shoulder messenger and still okay. I walk slowly. Pocket phone and zombie through security gate. Show guard my ID hoping he can see the fear in my eyes and arrest the angel of death stalking me, but he doesn't. Make it as far as the library and have a seat on the ice-cold slate in front of the bust of Martin Luther King Jr. I become aware of the inevitable and see two graduate students approaching. *Ask for help,* I command myself. This is it. My soul screams out of course, but I don't. I watch them pass. Take phone out to find hospital, and it dies. To my young readers: Don't be too cool to ask for help ever about anything. Especially if you're about to die before a bust of Martin Luther King Jr. Pocket my phone resigned to the inevitable. I lie back down and begin to let go. If you've never had an asthma attack, it's a surround sound of suffocation and misery. When your ears are plugged or filled with fluids you hear what's going on inside loud and clear. The more your immune system fights, the more your head fills with the fluids and the more fluids the more pressure. Eventually, if you're as foolish as I am, you'll find yourself with a hurricane between your ears and no place to rest. I'm transported temporarily back to when we were staying with Nora in Newington. Nora was an angel with a thousand cats. We'd been evicted twice and were lucky to have a roof over our heads at the time, so cats were the least of concerns, but they did me in good. It just so happened that my best friend, Timothy, popped up around the same time and came to visit us. He was in a transient phase himself, I believe, but we hadn't seen each other for years since Love Lane, and Timothy always had jokes. My inability to laugh/breathe only made it funnier to Timothy, who couldn't not be funny. I remember feeling drunk from laughing and lack of oxygen and Timothy not letting up in the slightest. Nana finally drove him home for fear I might die laughing. That was the last time I saw Timothy, I believe. He was shot to death in New Haven when I was away at boarding school. Guess I'm on my way now. *God.* I'm exhausted. *Please help.* I can't explain it any way other than a countdown of sorts. It's the strangest feeling in the world and a bit amusing, given the circumstances, until I realize it's my last breaths I'm counting and that I only have a few left. Each breath is clearly quieter and shorter until two and one and . . . I surrender to my new breathless state, gazing up at the sky with little left but a childlike curiosity. I surrender. Foolishly.

OTHER

1 / ALIVE

THERE'S NO LIGHT OR LIFE FLASHING BEFORE MY EYES. There's nothing really. There's a quiet calm, a gentle observation, and me waiting. That's it. I'm reminded as I'm lying on the ice-cold slate below the bust of MLK, assuming I'm either dead or on the other side, that I'm not breathing and thus breathing might not be so essential to me anymore. I look at the two stars you can see in a New City night sky and wait for something profound to tell me something. I wait until I begin to wonder what I'm waiting for. Spurred on by a new boredom of sorts, I sit up. I sit up and I look around. Nothing new to see or do, I remember I'm still without breath. Roll the dice and exhale. Confused and slightly afraid, I attempt to inhale. Not only do I exhale and inhale, but I breathe as if I never had an asthma attack in the first place. I stand up. I stretch in my newfound reality. The leaves! The fallen leaves smell so warm and full of life. How could I never have noticed before? They smell like toasted almonds and fresh-cut grass. My eyes well up. I touch the cold grass with my right hand, thank God, and hold my heart with my left.

2 / SPONTANEOUS

My phone's still dead, but I'm alive. Walk to the computer lab. I try every algorithmic variation of "asthma" + "attack" + "instantaneous" + "spontaneous" + "sudden" + "recovery." Nothing. Asthma kills ten Americans daily. I find that out.

The computer lab will be closing in fifteen minutes, a voice says over the intercom. *Please save or print your work.*

Close out all windows except my Word document. It's one thing to write about homelessness or education in society. It's another thing completely to recount a firsthand miracle. What in the world am I supposed to do with a miracle? Not that I'm not grateful. I'm super grateful. I'm just saying people have a hard time believing my life as is. Now I have to tack a present-day miracle onto that? I do my best to get the bones down, but it's not easy to remember the order of events because I was drunk and terrified the whole time. I document the wake-up and thugging the older lady for her seat and crawling up the steps and the two passing graduate students and my foolish pride and the final surrender. I walk to the restroom, wash my face, and kick off to the train. A glorious walk. I pass the security guard, and he's baffled. In New City when you're truly happy to be alive people's gut reaction is to call the cops on you. See a scribe taking a bite out a Big Mac on the steps I just crawled up. Pass and refill my card.

3 / F+

TRAIN TO THE CITY AND EXIT IN CHINATOWN. WALK aimlessly toward New City Bridge. Stop about halfway and lean over. Look at water. Another scribe will tell you how beautiful it is. I see the depth. I feel the power and the draw. I understand why people jump. Thankful to be me, I fold my hands and say a prayer for all.

Great night, stealthy suit says in passing.

It really is, I tell him. End up near Times Square spun around and lost in familiar places. I feel low again. Take two random lefts and find myself at the entrance of the Ram's Head Hotel. Push through. I don't know where else to go and I'm tired. I'm tired of thinking. Tired of walking. Tired of trying to survive New City winter alone. Tired of pretending I'm okay with the way things are. Time to do something stupid.

Welcome to Ram's Head, clerk says. *Do you have a reservation or are you booking a room with us tonight?* Look behind me for no good reason and an orange Ferrari roars past. I guess if I had to title this portion of the journey I'd call it *For No Good Reason.* Half the time I have no clue what I'm doing or why I'm doing it other than it's something I haven't done before. This time feels much darker.

Book please, I say. *Something with a view if you can.*

Let's see. We have a seventh-floor single, no smoking?

I nod yes and buttons get pushed.

Upgraded you to a double. Your total for one night is three hundred fifty-six dollars and eighty-three cents. How would you like to pay? Cash or—

Hand over my card.

Per-fect. Swipes. *Thank you, sir.*

Sir. I like that.

Anyone who spends four hundred bucks on a hotel room . . . Sir. He laughs.

Elevator up and key the door. I love hotels. I love the whole experience. I love the elevator up and the doors swinging open and the comfortable order of everything. I love the fresh linens and the lack of cats. I love the smell of the lotions and the rare city views. I love hotels and airports. It's a strange past-life affinity, I'm sure. Put my phone on charge and step out to balcony. Windy but nice. A plane inches across the cityscape. After a minute there are several. I wonder where people are going. Look down and watch the antlike street action. I'm drawn to it. Elevator down, excited, and see a new clerk at the desk. I can't place where I know him from, but he looks familiar. He laughs at the screen and I realize it's Dread from the Styleshop I stole the suit from. Keep my cool and carry on. Card overdrafted from room charge, I'm sure I'll find some free entertainment for the night. On cue, a streetwalker approaches a lady of the night.

Off the clock, darling. She cuts the conversation short.

Walker laughs. *If I had a Caddy, you'd be on my time.*

But you don't.

I see how it is. Walker lets her go. *Watch when I come back in a Maybach.*

Spell "Maybach," she says over shoulder.

Walker turns to a café. He pulls the door open and walks in with such a confidence you'd imagine he was a billionaire. I follow him just because he seems like the type of person you follow. Journal it as he orders a cup of ice from cashier.

Fifty cents. Cashier eyes me.

You charging me for ice now, Papa?

You think we get for free?

Walker shells over a quarter. *Take it or leave it, Aki.* He chews ice chips by the door and watches night life. Walker opens door for bus driver in hurry. Driver thanks him, cops a banana, orange juice, and an egg-and-cheese bagel. Look at the clock and it's 3:39 a.m. Walker chews ice. Just when I feel I've about worn out my welcome a woman crashes through the door and kisses Walker on the cheek. Eagle eye out, I peep her slide a fold of cash into his pocket. Perfect night to be adrift in New City. Driver pays for his breakfast sandwich and leaves with the woman.

You either a cop or weirdo, Walker says to me as he motions for a refill.

I'm a writer, I say. *Strange hours.*

I can dig it. You see things beyond the masks. Don't go too deep. He laughs. *You need some female companionship tonight, or you working on your novel?*

Novel.

We laugh.

Thank you, though.

Of course.

Then as if we've known each other all our lives we just sit there in the New City equivalent of silence. All three of us.

I bet your father was a preacher, I say to Walker.

His eyes bug. *You a cop!*

I have a friend in your line of work, and both his folks are ministers. It's a energy thing.

Makes sense. Walker grits his teeth. *For every action there's a reaction.*

A convoy of police cars flies by with sirens and lights. Then it's just us and the quiet again.

You got a day job? Walker asks me.

I'm a substitute teacher, I tell him.

Where at?

New City Public. It's in—

I know Public. I went to Art and Design. His eyes lock in on action outside. *Public is a great school,* he says. *Be right back.*

Wait for a bit and then get excited to head back to Ram's Head and lie in my bed. Pack up and kick off. On the approach I see I forgot about Dread at the desk. *Be cool,* I tell myself through the sliding doors.

Welcome to Ram's Head, he says.

Raise my room key.

Welcome back, I should say.

Thank you. Have a good night.

You too.

Stay cool and elevator up. Key door and step out onto balcony. See Walker and his foam cup below laughing with a couple cops.

Life is funny. Step back inside, wash up, and lie out on the bed like a starfish. Rest my eyes. Get excited about sleep but can't. Rise, dress, and head back downstairs. Walk away from the familiar until the sound of the city is behind me. I don't know how long I walk, and I left my phone at home, but I pass the point of wondering how long it will take to get back twice already. Before I know it, I'm on an expressway. After the eeriness there's a romantic quality to the wide road at night. Darkness and headlights. Few signs besides those absolutely necessary. Nothing else to keep one company. No doors to imply safety. Nothing but the sound of your own footsteps and the occasional vehicle. Approach an overpass with night lights and American flags tied high to the fencing on both sides. Shadowy figures underneath turn out to be an abandoned Corrona with orange stickers on the driver-side window and an Oldmobile. They're facing each other on one side of the road like someone needed a jump and last minute they both had to bail. I can't see much but for the second or so when a car flies by. My dunks are soaked from walking in the grass. I turn back.

4 / HEART

WELCOME BACK, DREAD SAYS.

You don't remembers me, do you?

I do. You were just here. He looks bemused.

I show him the lining of my blazer and he's even more confused.

You helped me pick this jacket.

Styleshop, he says. *That's closed now. Been closed.*

Word?

Word. That's how I ended up here. Had me on the front page of the Post.

If the sun wasn't rising, I'm sure I would have just believed him and went to sleep, but I walk over and enjoy the New City sunrise to see it for myself. Sure enough, the windows are blocked out with brown paper and painter's tape. That chapter's done. Catch a quick nap before checkout and use the side exit. Phone rings.

Junie?

It's my father. So strangely odd and familiar to be called Junie.

Pop. Pop's in Connecticut visiting Grandma Billings. Grandma Billings is Pop's mother, who raised me on Love Lane just as much as anyone. I remember her telling me to look both ways to cross the street and a young man should always have some money in his pockets and going fishing with the worms we caught and the smell of her mint gum and cigarettes and fried catfish. I remember Grandma Billings like it was yesterday all with the mention of her name, shocked that we grow to forget people so easily. I remember myself as little Junie. I remember the plastic over the carpet steps I used to slide down in my onesie and the tender kisses Grandma Billings gave me. Pop tells me she has late-stage brain cancer and it'll probably be his last visit. Hits me like a freight train.

We all knew this part was coming, Pop says. *It's been going on for a while now, so . . .* He can't hide the hurt in his voice. *It's time,* he says.

Man. I don't know what to say.

It's all been said, son. The reason I'm calling is because I got this rental car till tomorrow and my flight don't leave till late. What you got going on today? CT to New City take about an hour and forty. I drive more than that back and forth to work. If you free, I'm on my way.

I'm definitely free.

What's your address so I can put it in the GPS?

Texting it right now. Text the Murkt Street address. *Got it?*

Yeah, buddy.

I catch a break in the bouncy Park Avenue mob and walk to bookstore on Broadway. Wash my face and hands in restroom. Brush teeth. Peruse new art books and do some catch-up journaling. Let loose of the anxiety of ifs and thens, and come to terms with the present. It is what it is. People watch. Hundreds of drunken Santa Clauses march across Broadway. Parents shouldn't lie to their kids about Santa. Pack up and train back to Broadway Junction to meet Pop. Christmas trees line the street-sign island. Bus exhaust swirls in the fragrant pines. Make the walk to the old house, and phone vibrates on my approach.

Pop.

Man, you still walk the same. Pop pulls up to the house and double-parks. He hops out and we hug. Man. His face is my face. His build is my build. His posture. His smile. There's so much that I assumed my own—habits I couldn't have learned from Pop, body language, and speech patterns—which I now realize has very little to do with me. The laugh. The slur. The ways. Reuniting with your father after close to twenty years feels like finding a long-lost version of yourself. A prototype or a mirror image. I can only imagine what Pop feels. Heartwise, I've never felt so vulnerable and so safe at the same time. It's overwhelming. All may not be clear, permanent, or realistic, but all there is in this timeless moment is love. We catch up. Two decades is suddenly both a lot of time and almost nothing. I listen and tell him everything I can think of. We sit in his rental and reunite with each other but also with parts of ourselves that we didn't know had disconnected. It's impossible to describe properly because there's so much symmetry, implausibility, and magic. After our talk we walk to Maffia's for heroes and Pop hands a dollar bill to the scribe outside. It's a warm, sunny winter day.

Das you fadar? Maffia pushes the deli meat slicer back and forth.

Yes ma'am.

She nests the heroes in a paper towel and scribbles numbers on the wax paper. *Okay. See you later.*

We eat in the rental and people-watch. *My son the artist,* Pop says. *I'm proud of you, One.*

'Preciate that, Pop.

United Strays, huh? Scared to even think what you wrote about me. Not that I don't deserve it.

It's more a reckless year in college, really, I tell him. *I don't do too much reflecting in it.* Take a big bite. *I'm excited to hear what you think, actually.*

I'mma read it tonight, then. A police cruiser pulls up, looks inside at us, and wheels off.

So where's your old spot at? Pop asks. *Here?*

I point over his shoulder.

You miss it?

I do.

You should come on out to Cali. Come out west and regroup . . . or stack up, really. You could make a killing out there.

Man. I feel the palm tree breeze. *After I finish what I have to finish here, I'm on it.*

For real. Meka and Lil' Jay gonna trip when they see big bro. Pop takes a picture of me eating a hero. *That's a good flick too.* He shows me.

Dope. Landlord's old Cadillac pulls into the driveway. *Oh.* I jump out. *Let me see if I got any mail.*

Cool. Pop rolls his window down.

I step out as they're walking in through the side door. Run up and ring the bell. Hear the gate shaking as the landlord's wife opens the door.

I thought you was a Jehovah's Witness. She laughs. *I'll be right back.*

I will. Wave goodbye as he merges with Junction traffic. New City doesn't slow down for reunions or the process of emotions, but I feel it all. Although it's sad to see him leave, a part of me feels whole again for the first time in a long time. Train back to the city to the same bookstore on Broadway and try to write down the heart of it. I feel like I have to learn a whole new language to express myself now. I buy a new notebook with bread Pop blessed me with, stash the old one along with the great void I carried for decades, and relocate to a café. I scribe anew from what remains, which is almost everything and next to nothing. So strange to look back on the man I was literally yesterday with such contrast, distance, and clarity. Life is bugged out. Most people would rather cling to their pain-fueled memories than reconcile with positive change. Most would rather hang on to their identity than let love in. I was almost that. I can recognize and feel it still, and I'm so thankful I'm not. Writing out the heart of it, I come to see I've done a lot of spiteful things and had senseless warring with whatever, just begging for attention and/or recognition. I see other things too, but the spitefulness stands out. Perhaps it's my first time being able to see me. A fear grows in my stomach as I realize Pop's probably reading *Strays* right now. Stop writing and speed-read through it myself. *Phew.* Nothing too bad. There's one part where I mention him indirectly when I walked into the bottle. Bag *Strays* and fish through mail. Toss junk. Get a letter from Alcorn Correctional Facility in Mississippi. Aya. Open it up and read. Good to hear from him. Mixed feelings about his portrayal in *Strays,* but all in all he loved it. Said it was real and he's been writing too, which I realize is my ultimate goal. See a cocky pigeon hop the curb and peck at a half-eaten chicken wing. *Savage.* Pigeon eyes me. Last letter's a small heavy package. I tear it open and see a copy of *Strays* with a rejection letter. Disrespectful times a thousand. I kick off and follow my intuition toward the Westside Highway. *Beep! Beep!* Hear a horn, turn, and see Blue, Big, and Hollywood pulling up. *What's good, Black man?* Hollywood says.

Need a ride? Blue asks.

I hop in and do a round of daps and pounds.

Let me guess—you juuust finished debriefing the captain? Big.

I mean, the gang's all here. I deflect. *What this, a raid or a ride-along?*

Here you go.

Y'all know I'm not the rat.

That's what a rat says. Big wins the rat roast.

We all laugh. The boys are on their way to Row's, and I follow the movement.

You bounced mad quick the other day, Blue says.

I was having an asthma attack, I tell him.

We get to Row's and in no time we're having a heated debate about politics and the people. Nothing worth repeating here. Emotional and cyclical. Somehow the conversation switches to personal confidence, and I feel a new wholeness I've never felt before. I'm so detached from the argument that I couldn't care less who wins and don't say much.

When you confident, you comfortable. Hollywood instructs us on the subtle nuances of panache. *If you comfortable in your own skin and the camera's on, it's just natural. Everybody look good on camera.*

5 / OIL

A WOMAN FUMBLES A HEAD OF LETTUCE, WHICH ROLLS to our cart. I pick it up and return it to her.

Thank you, young man. Smiles.

Veggie mister hisses. Next aisle there's a mother of two reaching for a box of cereal.

Can you . . . ? she asks.

Help her too. *I don't know why they put these so high.* It's a reach.

Thank you, she says.

Aisle three I try a low profile. Aloof even.

A woman approaches. *Can you help me, please?*

We journey over to aisle ten.

Why's olive oil so expensive? Leslie asks upon my return, lobbing penne pasta into cart.

Our holiday coffee turned into last-minute shopping at the grocery store.

Should I get the big one? It's on sale.

Absolutely. I cart a half gallon for her.

I used to love the grocery store. It always felt like a field trip. Everything in the grocery store was always colorful and brand-new, and I'd always get a good nap on the way back. It was my first job on the Vineyard. Now I feel like a hostage to consumerism.

You can't do everything by yourself, June. Leslie coaches me on the work of being a writer. *It's a waste of time and energy, really. You have to let people help you so you can focus on the writing.*

I'm learning, I say.

Good time to do so. I know people who would love to work with you.

Leslie's not saying anything new, which makes it all the more powerful today. Today I'm fully open to it. First time probably. Sometimes you're so focused on your goals that you forget the basic, everyday baby steps. A lot of the times. Especially if you is me.

You know, I'm guest editing a literary magazine out the UK on experimental art, and I'd love to have them commission some of your pieces, if that's okay. I think your new work would fit great.

6 / HARLEM

WALK LESLIE HOME, HELP UNLOAD GROCERIES, AND head uptown to meet Hollywood and some of the basketball players at Harlem Bones.

Peanut never showed? I ask Hollywood.

Said he had to run errands for his father.

Hollywood calls for the bill. *You want to split it or . . . ?* He lets the question linger.

Or. I laugh.

It's not bad. He shows me. Just over a hundred dollars. We split the bill and dip off to meet A.U. in Sugar Hill. The boys thank us and carry on. At a certain point during the holidays New City clears out a bit and we get to bounce around with friends and family like a happy little village. We ride the strange wave like a magic carpet.

The thing is, Hollywood argues to the do-rag committee, *a lot of these kids don't have real men in they lives. A lot of them don't have fathers or mentors or nothing. If you a Black male educator, you a mentor whether you like it or not. You gotta accept that and be all in with it.*

These kids is so checked out, though, bro, Navy Do-Rag counters.

I ask if anyone knows anyone who's renting. They don't. Not at the moment. Ask folks to please keep an ear out.

No doubt, A.U. says.

I wouldn't let my girl wear some of these skinny jeans these cats is wearing, Red Do-Rag chimes in. *I don't get that wave.*

Everybody goes through that, A.K. says. *You ever look at old pictures of us?*

We laugh.

I'm dead serious.

A.K. walks to his room, pulls out our boarding-school yearbook, and returns. Something about the pictures of us at fourteen or fifteen and being in Harlem or the vibe of the conversation puts me in a kind of download daze, and I remember. Harlem. It hits me like a lightning bolt. A few terabytes in a flash. Much like remembering a dream upon wake-up, I can feel massive blocks of nostalgic power and detail slip away with each second. Take out my notebook and scribe what I can. I write for a half hour about Harlem. An older version of me would have told about the sudden memories and talked for a half hour. New me knows talking is not enough. Some things you must process for yourself. Yesterday's me would have talked about it and been triggered to steal something frivolous, as if the world owed me again. Today's me is grateful I'm with my heart and how it feels. Harlem. How could I forget? Harlem's the sole reason I came to New City in the first place. It was Harlem I fell in love with. Not New City. A.K.'s yearbook pictures reminded me of my Harlem dream deferred, crusted over and forgotten. Langston Hughes's words have proved prophetic, about and in Harlem. For years I have been in walking distance and I can't even remember the last time I thought to visit the very place that drew me to New City. Maybe that's what all my lonely drifting has been about. Forgot about my first love.

7 / 2010

END UP ON THE EAST SIDE IN THE FIFTIES STILL FEEL-ing brand-new. Stumble upon the most decadent New City dead ends I've ever seen, each lined with million-dollar mansions and waterfront park views. Hear the high-pitched whistle of a fire-cracker rise. It's supposed to be a full moon tonight. Walk inside the park. A second whistle screams up into the night sky—*Paaah!*—and an explosion of sizzling red embers reflects off the water. Find a bench and watch as dozens and then hundreds of red, purple, pink, green, white, yellow, and electric-blue explosives light up the night sky. A middle-aged couple approaches, smiles, and wishes me happy New Year.

I smile back. *Happy New Year!*

See three women hug each other and sing. Brook texts *Happy New Year* and says that we're throwing Nana a surprise party. Text back and follow the night into early morning. New City is quite a spectacle for the New Year celebration. I'll spare you the details, but it kept me up through the night to first light. And the next day.

Walk to New City Public, wash up, read paper, and prep for morning basketball. A few early birds show up, and I let them shoot around. Peanut enters gym with a wide smile and a break-fast tray.

Nah. He puts his tray down, walks up, and hugs me. *I OD missed you, Coach.*

"OD" means "a lot" or "very much so."

I was tight I couldn't make Harlem Bones.

I missed you too, Peanut. No food in the gym, though.

Got you. He tosses the tray. *I ate already anyways. Just being greedy.*

More morning ballers show up, and Peanut puts on his ball kicks.

Have a seat around the bulldog! I pass around a sign-in sheet and count heads. *Now, here's the thing,* I say.

Here we go. Peanut warns the new students.

Most of y'all think basketball is a game. And it is. Orange ball. Two orange goals. You play around with your friends, show off for girls, shoot senseless threes, whatever. Basketball's also a multibillion-dollar industry and, most important, a way up. Most of you, if not all of you, actually think you can play. I look around at the fearful and semi-confident faces. *Go 'head and dream. There's nothing wrong with that. Dream, but make sure as you're pursuing that dream that you know what your competition looks like. Make sure you know what they're doing while you're messing around with your friends trying to impress girls with senseless three-pointers. Make sure you know you want something that millions of other people want as well. In this sense, basketball is not a game at all. Your competition is dead serious.*

Here comes the kid-from-Serbia story. Peanut unlaces his sneakers to chuckles.

Right now there's a kid in Serbia, I continue. *Could be Croatia or*

Palestine or Madagascar. Don't matter. Right now there's a kid somewhere with a handmade ball and a bucket nailed to a tree. He wakes up before you, works out, works on his game, identifies his weaknesses. He eats healthy, works out again, keeps track of his progress. And when he goes to bed he's exhausted. Every day and every night. Over and over. Why? Because basketball's not a game for him. It's his way up. There's a kid in Coney Island, in the Lower projects . . . in every city in every country of the world, doing the same thing. The reality you'll inevitably face is, these are your competitors. It's only a few hundred spots in the league, and most of them are already occupied by superstars. It's no coincidence no one from New City Public has even played Division One basketball. Reality sets in. *Who's going to be the first? Who's willing to put that work in? That's who I'm speaking to. The rest of y'all have fun. I'm not knocking fun. All I'm saying is, whoever's ready to compete I'm here to help to the best of my ability. The rest of y'all can relax and enjoy morning basketball. Rules to the gym—*

Double doors swing open, and J. Luis and Hollywood step through.

Yoooo . . .

Daps and hugs.

What's goody? J. Luis asks.

Same old, man. Laying low, staying out of trouble.

I hear that.

How you, kid? I ask him.

You know me. J. Luis grabs a rock, shrugs, and shoots a long three. *Just tryna get in where I fit in.* He chases the rebound down and dunks it.

Students ask him to do it again.

One and done for me. He smiles. *Drink your milk, though. You'll be up there soon enough.*

We 'bout to hit the rock, Hollywood says. *Bros need a break for real. You rolling? Or you patrolling?*

Ha-haaa! Cover me real quick?

Do your thing.

I run downstairs to my supply closet, text Brook, and pack a bag. *Bring some paper towels?* she texts back. Elevator back up, and Hollywood is preaching.

Endure, he says. *But you also have to evolve.*

I sit and listen.

Change your situation or change yourself—so you can change your situation.

Can we ball? Peanut pleads. *Pleeeease?*

8 / SURRENDER

THIS IS WHY I JOURNAL. LIFE IS SO SNEAKY AND RIGHT beside you the whole time that if you don't write or make some other kind of effort to remember, it'll stay hidden in plain sight forever. I journal for Harlem so I don't forget again. I document my meathead tendencies in real time so I don't misremember being better than I actually was. I journal so the living is genuine to me.

As luck shall have it, Hollywood, J. Luis, and I end up taking the 6 train uptown to crash at A.K. and A.U.'s before the drive, and it's Harlem all over again. Walk Malcolm X and Little Africa and take in as much as I can. When we get to the building A.K. and A.U. are outside on the stoop. Both over six and a half feet tall and outspoken, A.K. and A.U. are impossible to miss.

Gentlemen. A.K. surveys the block.

What's goody?

We dap, sit a couple steps below, and settle into the uptown action. Unpocket my phone and check for Harlem apartments for rent online. Sense a new presence, look up, and a group in bright biggie jackets approaches. Yellow Jacket breaks away, pulls his hood down, and runs up on us.

Give me all your lesson plans. It's Peanut laughing and smiling big.

J. Luis and Peanut's goonies are still on high alert until J. Luis recognizes Peanut from the gym. Daps and pounds round one.

This my coach, Peanut tells his boys. Daps and pounds round two. *What y'all doing in Harlem?* he asks.

Crashing for the night, Hollywood says.

That's what's up. I'm running errands for my pops. Matter of fact . . . Peanut checks his watch. *I'mma catch y'all later. Pops don't play 'bout his wings.*

Friends laugh in agreement.

For real.

We walk inside, watch semi-pro basketball, argue about everything under the sun, and retire, 1:07 a.m. I arise early in an unnecessary panic and write it out till 6:21 a.m. I write what I see looking out the window and reminiscing on when I used to daydream in boarding school doing the same thing. Here I am. Not at all how I planned it. I write about running into Peanut and what an abnormally good heart he has. I write in Harlem finally. See an old bookcase knocked over out front with something taped to the bottom. *Naaah.* I lower my pen, look closely, and nearly jump out the window in excitement. Step into my shoes, wedge a copy of *Strays* in the door, and hit the steps. Fly down two flights and run into two gentrifiers moving a leather couch. *Excuse me.* I try to thug 'em, but no real way to pass, so all I can do is wait.

Sorry. The woman apologizes in passing.

No problem. I run, hit the doors, and see garbagemen carrying the bookshelf away.

No no no no no no no . . . I grab hold of it, and they put her down. *I forgot . . .* Check the bottom, and the money's gone. *What in the*— Spin on my heals and inspect the grounds all around.

Garbagemen are early-morning unaffected.

Walk back defeated, and the lobby door is of course locked. Wait for someone to let me in. Couple with the couch saves the day. I thank them, take the steps two at a time, table the magazine, and melt. Wake up to the buzzer.

Hullo? Hollywood answers.

Hi, is this Hollywood? Voice in the buzzer.

Who is this? he says.

It's meee.

Ebony. Hollywood buzzes her in and unlocks the door. *She riding up with us to her uncle spot.*

Sorry to wake you guys. Ebony walks in.

It's all good.

Good morning, she says.

Morning.

The fellas finish packing up, and we head out.

We got everything? I hold the door open. *Wallet, keys, phone?*

Almost forgot. Hollywood doubles back. *Toothbrush.*

We hit the road, and it all becomes a blur. Suddenly, I'm the most tired man in America. I wake up and J. Luis is driving. Rise at a tollbooth and notice the clouds as we pass through. Come to in the middle of an argument about Obama and Black history. Consciousness. Pass out. Open eyes slowly to miles of colorful graffiti kaleidoscopes on highway rockland. Wake up, and we're parked between two eighteen-wheelers waiting for God knows what at a closed weigh station in Rye. The sky's now dark blue.

Son. Hollywood kicks the tires. *You was out like a light.*

You know you sleep with your eyes open? Ebony asks.

All the drifting and writing in lieu of sleeping and crashing wherever and light napping finally caught up with me. We meet J. Luis's people and highway on. Wake up to cop lights rolling behind us. Sit up and barely get to get concerned before the cruiser speeds off ahead.

What happened? I ask.

Nothing, Hollywood says. *Go back to sleep, bro.*

9 / TWELVE

WAKE UP AS WE'RE PULLING INTO THE STEAMSHIP parking lot. Pass out as we're driving onto the ferry and rise to crossing the Vineyard Sound. It's pretty amazing to wake up in a car on a boat floating weightless across the ocean. Wake up and we're crossing the bridge in Vineyard Haven. Wake up and we're wheeling up the sand-and-dirt road to our little house in the Highlands. I'm home. Rave, Rock, Henry, Uncle Willburn, Debs, Jennifer, Ev, E., Brook, and Nana are out on the porch.

Wake yo ass up, boy! Rock belly laughs. *Remember when Junie used to sleep in the car after the grocery store?*

Everyone falls out laughing. I open my door and say peace to the fellas. There are five or six conversations going on, and I catch none of it. Hug and kiss Nana a happy early birthday.

You knew, didn't you? Nana pinches me.

Before I can answer, Brook asks Nana if she remembers Floyd from Houston Street and the conversation dovetails. I forget how competitive conversations can be in my family. If you're not fast, loud, or funny, chances are no one's listening to you. You can try, buuut . . . Folks suggest Nana should write a book after one of her Love Lane stories, and she laughs.

I ain't writing no book. She's almost disgusted by the idea.

Even though I write religiously, it's refreshing to hear. Purple jeep pulls up, and Puda hops off his bike. Ma steps out the passenger side.

Aunty Mimi! Annie and Puda run up and hug her legs.

She looks great. This is home too. After the grilling and laughing it's a little chilly out, and people cram back inside. Nana and I stay out and watch the birds playing in the trees. Appreciate the last light and the quiet.

Blue jay. She points. *Beautiful.*

I realize in that very moment that I get my love of nature from Nana, and she gets it from Bear Paw, and he got it from whatever miraculous being carried us along to today. The blessing of the present man. Thank you, God. The sun sets and we walk inside together arm in arm.

Wait! Rock yells. *I said you can either leave on your own will—you know, out the door you just came in—or I can personally escort you out the window.*

Wait, wait, waaait! Ma can't stop laughing. *Wait . . . Wait . . . Phew . . . Remember when Grandma Billings shot Chief in the face?* She folds over.

And he was sitting on the curb looking like a lost puppy? How could I forget? Rock shakes her head. *I called the ambulance.*

I fetch the rake out the closet. Get a text from Hollywood that Big and Blue just got off the boat and 'bout to roll to Pequot. Tell him I'll meet them after I rake these leaves.

Make sure you check yourself good for ticks, Nana says.

I will.

So much changes so fast and so much life happens that I want to write it out as I'm used to, but somehow raking leaves feels far more important than any remembrance of ideas. Also, if it's worth remembering, I tell myself, I'll remember. I bag up the leaves as Puda runs alongside his bike and jumps on, butt-first, steering wild until his feet find pedals.

Uncle Willburn opens the kitchen window and talks through the screen. *That boy's a genius,* he says.

Um-hmm, Nana agrees. *He saw one of his friends do it, and he picked it right up himself. Just like that.*

Good for him, Uncle Willburn says.

It's difficult to pedal up enough speed on the bumpy dirt road, but if you run with the bike and jump on the seat, you can pedal into balance.

Nana chuckles. *He just as batty as you, June.*

I was always an adventurous kid.

Was he bad? Uncle Willburn instigates.

I wasn't that bad, I say.

I was surprised you made it past twelve, honey, Nana says frankly.

Wash my hands and walk through the historic Highlands toward town. Just like that, the fog has taken over. It's a dreamy type of night. Hit Pequot and front-porch it with Mom and Pop Dukes. Big and Blue's parents. Hell, they're like my parents too at this point. I wouldn't know New City had they not taken me in ten years ago.

Yer, Big says from the upstairs balcony.

Aaay. I walk upstairs past one of my old paintings and step out.

Hand me that book, Big says.

Close that door. Blue.

The mist plumes curl up into bright Van Gogh balls in front the streetlight with some fractal patterns I'm not smart enough to name just yet. We watch the tourists walk Pequot from the hotel to the Inkwell and back. This is home too. One of Big and Blue's young cousins comes up on a dozen lobsters for the low, Pop Dukes chefs it up, and we feast. I hate the tourism and seasonal entitlement, but I love the salty air of magic and sea. The trip is never long enough.

I walk home in the moonlit fog dodging skunks and rabbits and melt on the couch. Rise in the morning, shower, and it's time to go. The boys scoop me and we wheel to Vineyard Haven. The ferry back feels heavy. Depressing. Rain and high wind don't help. Determined not to feel sad or defeated, I pick up some bogeys to sell before we hit the highway. I'm kind of looking forward to the city. Nod out again and wake up to a text asking if I want to work the whole week next week. Hold off on my response. That's a kind of big commitment for a text message. Need to hear some details first. If you're not careful out here, you can walk right into a regular nine-to-five, which is more like death than you know. Pass out again and rise at a tollbooth. Catch the rock graffiti in entirety. I wonder how many people know about Bob Moses. He made New City. And the highways. Wake up to the city skyline shortly thereafter and the reality of my nomadic existence.

Where you want me to drop you? Hollywood asks.

Uuuh. Run through my options: Gold Street is a no-go since

I'm still traumatized from my asthma attack and everyone's on the Island, Row's out of town for work, and I'm in no shape to party. *What time is it? Any train'll do.*

Hollywood wheels up to a 6 station. *You can crash at my spot if you want. It ain't nothing.*

Oh, I'm good for tonight, I front. *Good-looking, though.*

You sure?

Feels like he can sense the bull.

Yessir.

I bag up, kick off, and descend back down into New City underground. Catch the 6 train downtown and ride back and forth feeling like basura, straight trash. Surface, catch a twenty-four-hour café, and write it out as best I can. For such a short trip so much came up out of me. I journal about watching the birds play with Nana and realizing the grace of our existence. It's pure gold. The way I see it, reuniting with my father has given me new eyes with which to view the world and I'm now realizing I've been sitting on a field of diamonds all along. We aren't the richest in terms of money, but I'm surrounded by some of the wealthiest souls in the world. I spent so much time in angry-orphan-artist mode, I couldn't recognize the blessings right up under me. I was raised on a field of diamonds and protected by hearts of gold. Least I can do is pay my penance in words and ride the night to first light.

Hit the school early, bust a Spartan shower, and pass out in the gym for an hour before morning basketball. Wake up filled with an inexplicable adrenaline and survey the dark, quiet gym. Nothing. Realize as my energy wanes that I had one foot in a wild dream still running from a tiger on rickety rooftops. Rise and open up for morning ball. Drop a brief gem from Dr. Wooden about putting your socks on properly and let the boys play. Sub gym, one block of statistics, and head toward the hellevator for good old middle school lunch duty. Wait quietly with some early birds, trying my best not give in to the feelings of nausea and anxiety. Maybe this is what the tiger dream was about. Foreshadowing. A high school class descends the back staircase and passes with little to no friction. So far so good. Could it be that my touch-a-wall strategy is actually working? Elevator doors slide open and it's peace and quiet. *If I can hear you when I come back down,* I load the first group, *you don't get to ride. Tell your friends. Touch a wall and be quiet. Easy-peasy.*

Aside from some inevitable randomness, computer carts, and pseudo-emergencies, I manage the back elevator for middle school lunch. Elevator down one last trip. No students in sight.

Laaast trip, I yell.

Hold it! Don turns the corner. *Thanks, man.*

No problem. Where you headed?

It becomes clear to me after a week or so that I may have overachieved with the elevator duty. Staff and students start using the back as a first option.

10 / DIG

GRANDMA BILLINGS PASSES AWAY. IT'S A HEARTBREAKER. How do we forget about people? People who mean so much to us? What good is striving in life if we forget what matters in the process? I did get to see her before she transitioned, and by the time I got there they'd already stopped feeding her. Food was more trouble than it was worth at that point. I regretted not visiting sooner as soon as I saw her.

She saw me and said, *You just now seeing me?*

The woman who took me fishing and cared for me so tenderly. I'm not sure I can muster up the words to express how it affected me.

As fate shall have it, Brook calls me shortly thereafter, crying, saying Nana's unresponsive and being flown off-Island for emergency surgery in Boston.

I'm on my way, I tell her. Coordinate with Joy and book the first bus out. Joy and I meet up at the hospital and find the intensive care unit just as they're wheeling Nana through on a stretcher. She's unconscious but stable, they say. Nothing we can do except pray and wait as they figure out what happened. Joy and I lived through shelters, senseless violence, trauma, addicts, and addiction. As if we were being prepped for something greater, we experienced a lot of life's dark underbelly at early ages. As heavy as some of it was, for better or worse it made us steady. Nana undergoes multiple surgeries but recovers well. Joy and I book a hotel room and settle into the unknown. It feels strange doing so, but we go out and find a quiet restaurant to eat. I wonder to myself, journaling in the hotel room afterward, if I'd have jumped on a bus so fast had I not felt the pain of my absence with Grandma Billings. I definitely felt something bigger than me take over when Brook called and my response was automatic. *I'm on my way.* There was no question.

The morning staff lets us see Nana, but she's still knocked out. We're getting a positive update from the team of doctors working with her, pretending like we understand their terminology when Nana starts moving again. The nurses hustle over and talk her back to consciousness. She's confused but struggling to clarity. Her eyes find me.

Voice nearly gone, she whispers, *What happened?*

Joy and I spend the week in Boston with Nana as she recovers. Turns out it's her favorite hospital. One of the best in the country. Perfect place for a person like Nana to regroup. She and the other nurses trade war stories. Most she likes. Some she don't. A priest comes regularly and says prayers. The day comes, and we see Nana off on her journey back to the Island. Joy and I go our separate ways. If you looked past the constant beeping of critical machinery and a cold, clinical smell, the hospital felt like an asylum of love. My weeklong trip to Boston hurt the pockets but filled the spirit. It also gave me time and space to revisit all of whatever this is. I wanted to be a writer so I could write about romantic rendezvous and adventures. Life had other things planned. In hindsight I may have made a few changes here and there, but all in all this is me. You can't change one decision without affecting the rest of it, and this is learning on the fly. I'm okay with the fact that I'm as true to me as I can possibly be, and there's a small honor in that. Writing's the easy part. I revisit months of not knowing what tomorrow will bring fueled by odd intuitions and a half-a-million-dollar thinker. I cry remembering Grandma Billings. I wonder if the journey's worth the ink. I revisit all the things that I've forgotten in pursuit of something I can hardly remember. It reminds me to slow down and how sometimes just being there is invaluable. I revisit my miracle. My God. How does a miracle sit somewhere above the cupboards collecting dust? Even addressing it here to my own self, it still feels a bit untrue. Too rare to share. Spontaneous events of magnitude do not vibe well with everyday reality, so those of us called upon to be writers learn to filter it through fiction. I revisit pages that kept me up at night. Fueled by decaf coffee and another frivolous hotel stay, I revisit all of this again and it feels a lot like what needs to be said.

11 / NIGHT

I'M SUBBING GYM FRIDAY AND IT'S LAST PERIOD. WE
play Utah.

Yo, Coach, A. says. *You should dead coach us next year.*

"Dead" is a qualifier; the nearest English equivalent would be
"definitely" or "seriously."

I am coaching you next year, I tell him.

Dead ass?

Yessir.

Oh, it's a wraaap. He celebrates by shaking Young Chris, who
hates to be touched.

Last period and the weekend upon us, we play one more game
of Utah and talk playoffs and college ball. The conversation drifts
from the nuances of the game to self-awareness and quantum phys-
ics. I realize these aren't teenagers at all. Somehow I'm always surrounded by magic people. It's amazing to me what they've already
considered at sixteen and seventeen. Black matter, déjà vu, connec-
tivity, synchronicities—ideas that don't have a place in everyday
conversation, let alone school. Conversations that arise when the
school year's winding down and it's Friday last period and instead

of racing for the finish line people are quietly reconsidering the trajectory of it all.

'Cause boom. We're here chilling having this conversation, A. says. *Meanwhile we whipping around the sun at a hundred and seventy-seven thousand miles per hour. You ever been in a car doing a hundred? We doing more than a thousand times that.*

And that's just our universe, Miles says.

And yet we hardly feel a thing. Cudi pushes into his shoe.

Hollywood suggests we step out for a slice before Bravos gets crazy. My phone buzzes.

Hellooo, darling, Nana sings.

Hey, Nana.

How you doing, sweetheart?

I'm great. 'Bout to grab some pizza. How you doing?

I'm just wonderful, she says. *Chilling in the West Wing, enjoying the sun, and the birds are putting on a show to— Hold on, June. Who is it?*

I hear Nana stand from her recliner.

Hold on, honey. Somebody's at the door. See who that is, Puda.

It's a white guy! Puda yells.

Must be Meals on Wheels. Hellooo? Hold on, June, Nana says.

Hear a muffled conversation.

. . . can't be a coincidence. June? the voice says through the phone.

Who's this? All my student loans flash before my eyes. Credit cards forged in my name. Thefts. The blazer. The hotel room(s) I overdrafted on.

This is Chris. I work for Junior. Is this really June?

Who?

Chris. I work for Junior.

He tells me Junior wants to meet me. He heard about me from such and such, and he happened to be on-Island and looked me up in the phone book. Martha's Vineyard is one of the rare places left with billionaires who can change your life in a second and a local phone book.

Who was that? Hollywood dabs the oil from his slice with a napkin.

You not even— I almost say. Almost. The words and the excitement are right there, but I take a bite of my slice instead. *Best pizza in the city.*

You buggin'. Hollywood shakes garlic powder and oregano over his plate.

Who's better?

Bang-for-your-buck-wise?

You tell me.

If we factor in cost efficiency, you gotta put Three Bros in the discussion.

That's a fact.

Big and Blue hit us up and say they're at Q.'s in Stytown, so we walk over and take in the city. Everything is so bright and alive. You can feel the summer vibes coming alive in New City. We play the living room with the boys and watch mindless television. Blue turns to Junior's Actors Guild interview.

Wait, Q. says. *I love this guy.*

I don't say anything. The urge is there, of course, and my ego almost betrays me, but I keep it to myself. As difficult as it may be, I've learned that certain moments in life are for you and you alone. The key to keeping your mouth shut is to not say anything for a day. Once you can do it for a day, you can do it for how-ever long you need to. Friday festivities pull us into the night like a pack of wolves, each searching for our glorious rewards. I don't find much, but I do luck up on a crash on a couch not my own with friends who feel like family and a morning to look for-ward to. The city feels far more personal Saturday mornings. They might be my favorite. I rise, brush my teeth, wash up, and head out early for my meet.

Lady runs up to traffic cop. *That guy's standing there pulling his pants down!*

Traffic cop isn't too concerned.

You don't even care, do you?

Traffic cop smacks his teeth and waves a truck down Third. Lady storms off and I wait for the light. Cross, sign in with build-ing security, elevator up, and introduce myself to the secretary, Madison.

You're early, she says.

Yeah. Sorry about that.

Don't be. You can have a seat.

She goes back to reading her article. It's a piece about an award-winning photograph that recently went viral. I read it re-cently myself, and I can't help but pick her brains about it.

You should feel bad, she says to me. *But in a good way.*

She's talking about society and how most of the people who care are more or less powerless to make real change. That's what I take from it anyway. Some white women speak in a way where I'm not sure if their words are connected with their hearts. It's just brains computing. It terrifies me. It's as if she's saying I should care because everyone else now cares. Leslie sent me the photo and the piece last week, and we more or less landed on the same principles of humanity.

If the photographer is at any fault for taking the photo, we're also guilty for sharing in it, I argue.

Madison snatches her magazine back. *False.* She frowns in exaggerated disappointment.

If you haven't already seen it, the photo is a midrange shot of a starving child buckled over as if praying in barren lands with an opportunistic vulture watching on. The child was on her way to a food drop, and the photographer took the photo hoping the vulture would at some point spread its wings. What makes it so sad as an image is how clearly defeated the child is. How weak. How young and how worn down. She's starving to death. After the photo and the food drop, not much is known. The photographer made sure the child survived the journey and went on to witness many more man-made atrocities. Like I said, five million children under the age of five starve to death every year. Million. The photographer committed suicide, citing in his final note money problems, haunting memories, anger, and pain. The wrong people kill themselves for the wrong reasons all the time in this world of ours. This is life too. Junior Reid walks in.

Hey, June.

We shake.

Junior. Pleasure to meet you.

No, no. Pleasure's all mine. Thanks for taking time out of your day.

Junior's clearly in a rush.

Feel like I know your life story already. He smiles. *You're not afraid of flying, are you?*

No. Why?

No reason. He waves me to the stairs, which lead to the roof, which leads to a mars-black helicopter.

I'm a little worried about the blades! I'm ducking. *So close to my neck!*

Don't be! You have a higher chance of getting struck by lightning than decapitated by a helicopter blade!

We strap in with headsets, and the pilot lifts off, banking right toward Brooklyn. Tear a loose thread from my lining.

Time for a new blazer, huh?

Nah. I'm in style now.

Yeah? What style is this?

I call it Black grunge. Check my watch. *I can't tell you how many times I've sat right there at the Promenade and watched these things fly back and forth.*

It's a great way to get around the city. It's like the train for rich people. He shrugs. *So your story's amazing. You're a super talent and you're not a maniac. What's the catch? What am I missing? Why aren't you famous already?*

My credit score?

Get a chuckle out of the pilot.

Seriously! Junior picks back up. *You should be crushing it. Are you shy or something? Too humble? I bet you're too humble.*

I hate asking for help. I don't know. I think if you were Black, you'd be able to understand it a little better.

Really?

Oh yeah.

In this day and age that's disheartening. Junior signals for the pilot to take us down. *I have another meeting that was supposed to start five minutes ago, but . . . let's figure out what we can do to get you where you need to be. People need to hear your story.*

I agree. Take in the views. *Wait, how'd you even . . .*

My cousin pulled you over. He said you bribed him with a novel. I'm just kidding. He told me you gave it to him for free and that I should read it. So I did. I don't think there's a story like this out there. I mean, I'm a rich white man and you nailed the college experience for me. How that makes sense I don't know.

It's just real.

That makes sense. The rest is mostly Google. You're not hard to find.

Pilot drops me off on the roof and goes back to wherever pilots and rich people come from.

June! Madison the secretary catches me from a ducky door and raises a small manila envelope with my name on it.

We hug goodbye and I kick off. Inside the envelope there's twenty-five bucks and a business card for Reid's Tailoring with the words *Cab fare* written on the back. I raise my hand and cab over, knowing the universe likes immediate action and I literally have nothing else to do. It's not the right usage, I know, but it sounds better to me. Reid's is a narrow, mirrored establishment wedged between a shoeshine and a Kinky's near or in Chinatown. An older gentleman is sitting up front at a dusty computer. Upon entering, I say hello and hand him the business card.

I hope this is the right place, I say. *Junior sent me.*

Sixty-ish, Sicilian-looking, the older gentleman hops to and begins pulling a measuring tape across my shoulders.

You get this suit near here? he asks.

No, I say. *Chelsea.*

Styleshop?

Yessir. They're closed down now, though.

He does that under-the-chin finger flick Bird used to do and proceeds to tell me a wild story of Russians, mobsters, escorts, and gambling.

It's always the debt that gets them. Okay. He goes back to dusty computer. *Come back tomorrow.*

That's it?

Until tomorrow.

Feeling high off life and not willing to let loose a bit, I walk to Asian Public for some dollar fries. I'm proud of myself. Get a text on cue and migrate with the boys to a house party in Brooklyn. There's the regular adventures and the crushes and belly laughs. It's someone's birthday, and we all go up two flights to the rooftop for sheet cake and fireworks. I realize looking at the New City skyline that I haven't journaled in days. I let it be. I'll catch up when I can.

Feel like death in the morning. Sun's obtuse. Brush teeth, wash up, and train to Reid's. Door closes behind me and cowbells chime.

I finished your novel. Reid ascends a stairwell out of the cave of mirrors with an armful of fabrics. *I have so many questions.* He pins slabs together around my torso and types at his computer. *Come back after lunch?* Hands me some chicken scratch on a paper.

Sure.

Say one thirty.

Okay.

Reid removes his reading glasses. *You know how many offers I've had for this place?*

I start to guess.

I can't even count, he says. *This is technically Tribeca. You know why I never sold? Why I still work? I love what I do. It's the key to life. Love what you do.*

How does one love making suits?

Reid taps his pointer finger to his temple. *You shall see.*

To kill time before lunch, I walk. I don't make it far. My head feels like it's going through childbirth. Float around Chinatown and Little Italy. My phone rings. Maggy asking for me to cover gym last two periods for full-day pay. Text her back yes. Easy money. I watch league ball at West Fourth, chess in Washington Square, and head back over to Reid's.

You ready? He's excited. Reid runs downstairs and returns with a suit and a shirt. *We need a tie for you too.*

If you say so. I grimace. *Sorry. Hangover.*

Late night? Reid asks.

Very.

I know just the fix.

Reid puts the suit away and we cab it to a restaurant/café a few blocks away named Rosa's.

How's the consommé? Reid asks the manager/server.

The squash this time of year. She kisses her fingertips.

I'll have that for me. Reid grabs my wrist. *My friend will do the chicken soup. The best,* he assures me. *They fry the neck up.*

Manager/hostess/server brings our meals and Reid sweet-talks her into a kiss on the cheek. The soup really is good. My headache's nonviolent.

That was amazing, my love, he says. *Compliments to the chef.*

She smiles, replies in Italian, and brushes the table off. The manager's walking away and Reid pats her on the butt for the only stare-down. He puts both hands up like he's innocent.

That's how you go to jail, I warn him.

Charges won't stick. Reid laughs. *That's my wife. This is Rosa's.* He smiles proud and then turns serious. *Never eat where you don't know the owner.*

I agree and draw a red feather on the paper napkin. No wonder I felt like I was eating in the kitchen. A waitress walks in, in a hurry. Late it seems. Everybody's in a hurry in New City. Even on Sunday. Waitress drops her purse and jacket behind the hostess station, and I see it's the girl with the black heart tattoo behind her ear from our last night at 1497 Murkt Street.

12 / STAR

I CATCH UP IN MY JOURNAL AND READ A NOVEL IN
Center Park with the great sun cooking my jeans. Bookmark the
page with my Saint Timothy flight stub and nod off in the sun.
Rise and watch a squirrel claw up a treasure out the dirt. A lot
happens that I thought was important, which it turns out doesn't
matter much now that I have time to reflect on it. See a young lady
dribbling and driving on the far court. Leave my blazer on bench
and walk over.

You hoop? I ask her.

Yeah. She shoots a deep three. *You a coach?*

*Yes ma'am. I was over there on the bench. What's all the dribbling
for? You get extra points for that?*

She handles the rock around her notebook and pulls up midrange. *If I can get to the bucket, it's two or three.* She can't be more
than twelve.

A good first step can get you to the bucket, I tell her. *You did your
homework yet?*

No waaay.

Do your homework. You can't play ball without grades.

She speed dribbles behind her back and shoots. Cash.

Homework should be illegal, she says.

Student-athlete, I remind her. *"Student" comes first.* I see Nana and Grandma Billings in her. I see Nana's heart and Grandma Billings's grit.

You played ball? she asks.

I played in high school and college, I tell her. *Division Three, though.*

What's that? she asks.

The best players play Division One or Two. The rest play Division Three.

She does the Shammgod with both hands. *I play for my church league.* Behind-the-back series. *And school.* Shot.

Oh, you ballin'. Chase down her rebound. *You play for two teams. But do you have a left hand?*

Double crosses. *I'm lefty.*

She shoots a long three and gets her own rebound. I clap for the ball and she sends a crisp chest pass. There's a nick under her right eye and a flesh wound like mine on her forehead.

Until you can do everything with both hands, you only half a ballplayer. I lead her with a bounce pass. *Let me see you finish with your right.*

She does it no problem. Something about kids with scars. They learn different. Everything sticks.

I'm going to go get a water. You want something?

A coffee if they have it. She shoots a pull-up.

You know coffee is a drug? I laugh.

I know. Caffeine. My grandma lets me drink it.

You Dominican?

No.

I'll get you a water if you want, I say.

Okay. I jog across the grass to hot dog vendor and cop two waters. Grandma Billings gave me some great advice when I was young, which for whatever reason I'm reminded of now. She was smoking at the dining room table and a roll of ash fell atop it. Grandma Billings caught my eye and told me in her Black, Great Migration rasp never to wipe ash away. She then blew the roll into her palm and dumped it into an ashtray. I walk back across the grass, and Star's shooting free throws. Hand her her water.

You know why I think homework should be illegal?

'Cause you don't want to do it, I say.

No. Take someone such as myself. She bunny-ears her laces. *Teacher don't know what my home life is like. I could have a little brother to care for or be sharing a room with my aunt or just have people always in and out the house. I might not ever be able to find a quiet place. Let alone for an hour and a half. How am I supposed to compete with the rest of the kids?*

I think about it. I'm convinced.

You thought I was buggin', right? Star tosses her water bottle in the bin and picks the rock back up. *And I like school.* She bombs a three. *School should just be more understanding.*

I dap Star and fetch my blazer. *You got a bright future ahead of you, young lady.*

I appreciate that.

I appreciate you. Keep following your gut. You got a good heart, I can tell.

I kick off toward the sun and let it all sink in. Look back to the courts as I approach the gate and see Star running wild like the wind.

Lock that left hand! I yell.

I hate stats, but a genius did some interesting math I read recently. Genius determined the odds of our family trees branching out to us through ages, plague, famine, war, disease, and so on. The odds of us evolving from stardust to language-speaking survivors of all today. The odds are one in three trillion. I say a prayer for Star. I pray that she aims for other goals. I pray that she remembers the basket is one way of scoring and not the only way. I pray Star remembers we're actually the breathing dust of stars. It sounds odd, but it's quite easy for us to forget. We get so caught up in the goals and aspirations or opinions of others that we sometimes forget the magnificence of just being. What else need there be? I pray that she envisions a future so brilliant the views alone make each and every valley worth the trip. I pray Star flies forward into the winds of adversity with such virtue and moxie that her wings'll burn forever red. I pray she journeys so far out of her comfort zone that she returns with only the most essential traits. I pray for her patience. I pray for her mind. I pray Star finds comfort in her truths and uncertainties. I pray that, regardless of what's ahead, she finds her way. What else? I pray she finds a place to do two hours of homework, because this world is still cold. I pray Star realizes and never forgets that those homes we tend to long for live ultimately in us.

My name's June Papers. I'm a New City substitute teacher. When they need me.

ACKNOWLEDGMENTS

This work would not have been possible without many people and places that made and/or saved me. I'd like to thank the dozens of mentors (friends), thousands of students (teachers), hundreds of books (portals), masses of families, and all the lovers who kept a light on along the way. There's not enough space here to credit and name you all but thank you. Thank you. Thank you. Thank you. IYKYK. In the words of the OG, "What's understood don't need to be explained."

Originally from Hartford, Connecticut, **JAMES W. JENNINGS** is an artist and educator with a BA in English from Emory University and an MFA from CUNY–Brooklyn College. He worked for many years as a substitute teacher and dean of students within the NYC Department of Education, taught English at Martha's Vineyard Regional High School and Martha's Vineyard Public Charter School, and is currently an internship coordinator/teacher mentor.